A Gangster's Syn 3

Lock Down Publications and
Ca$h Presents
A Gangster's Syn 3
A Novel by J-Blunt

A Gangster's Syn 3

Lock Down Publications
P.O. Box 870494
Mesquite, Tx 75187

Visit our website
www.lockdownpublications.com

Copyright 2019 by J-Blunt
A Gangster's Syn 3

Lock Down Publications
Like our page on Facebook: Lock Down Publications @
www.facebook.com/lockdownpublications.ldp
Cover design and layout by: **Dynasty Cover Me**
Book interior design by: **Shawn Walker**
Edited by: **Lauren Burton**

Stay Connected with Us!

Text **LOCKDOWN** to 22828 to stay up-to-date with new releases, sneak peeks, contests and more...

Submission Guideline.

Submit the first three chapters of your completed manuscript to ldpsubmissions@gmail.com, subject line: Your book's title. The manuscript must be in a .doc file and sent as an attachment. The document should be in Times New Roman, double-spaced and in size 12 font. Also, provide your synopsis and full contact information. If sending multiple submissions, they must each be in a separate email.

Have a story but no way to send it electronically? You can still submit to LDP/Ca$h Presents. Send in the first three chapters, written or typed, of your completed manuscript to:

LDP: Submissions Dept
Po Box 870494
Mesquite, Tx 75187

DO NOT send original manuscript. Must be a duplicate.

Provide your synopsis and a cover letter containing your full contact information.

Thanks for considering LDP and Ca$h Presents.

J-Blunt

Chapter 1

The conference room smelled like money, literally and figuratively. Seated around the twenty-foot mahogany table were twelve men of different ages, races, and religions. The one thing they had in common was they were all rich. Millionaires. Another thing they had in common was the serious look plastered on each of their faces as they listened to the man at the head of the table. He was an imposing figure, standing six-foot-four with a solid build, cocoa butter complexion, and silky black hair he wore in a ponytail, which told of his mixed heritage. The black, tailored suit with onyx cufflinks and soft-bottomed, hand-sown ostrich shoes said he was a man with fine taste.

"Gentleman, I assure you I have given a lot of time, attention, and consideration into this matter. This is a win-win for us all. I know nothing in this world is guaranteed except death, but I assure you no one will lose a single penny. This business venture will make us all richer and happier."

Silence filled the room as the tall, handsome man in the black suit stood before his audience watching the twelve powerful men's facial expressions. Some were caught in deep thought while others seemed to just stare, like they were sizing him up or evaluating his worth. The speech-giver stood poised, waiting for the questions he knew would follow.

"I must say, Mr. Reign, you certainly have a large pair of *cojones* to call us all together in one room to give this 'presentation'. You know we don't allow outsiders into our organization. We are secret for a reason, and we've had so much success because we keep secret. If the wrong people find out about us, things could end badly for us. You summoning us like this is a violation," an older Mexican man spoke, running his index finger and thumb across a bushy mustache. "But I don't mind taking risks every now and then, and I like a man who will do the same. He who risks nothing has nothing. Sure, he may get by, but he doesn't grow, change, or do anything memorable."

"Thank you for your words, Mr. Sanchez," Mr. Reign smiled, showing the dimple in his right cheek. "My father taught me that calculated risks must be taken from time to time if a man wants to improve his lot in life. Obviously you and Pop drank from the same fountain of wisdom."

Another man spoke. He was middle aged and dark-skinned with strong African features and a heavy accent. "I'm afraid I will not be so easily swayed, Mr. Reign. I won't trust you just because I've seen you on TV and you speak well and dress nice. That is how Mother Africa became a harlot to the Europeans. What is your gain? Since I've been here, I've only heard what we will gain. What about you?"

Mr. Reign's face became stoic as he locked eyes with Sakandu Obendowi. Then, very slowly, the light-skinned man's lips began to form a smile. "A man with a vision was the best thing that happened during the civil rights movement, and the worse thing that happened for people who believed in segregation in the U.S. Only a man with a vision can look at a tree and see a house. My vision, Mr. Obendowi, is to create a service that will allow me to become the most powerful man on the eastern seaboard while delivering quality service to those I do business with. My gain will be your gain. This meeting is about money and power. And if you want more of either, you'll see my vision is the way."

The African's face remained neutral, but the smile in his eyes said Mr. Reign had won him over. And as the opportunist glanced around the room, he saw the same look in the eyes of the rest of the men at the table.

"Two million dollars a crate is a lot of money. Twenty guns for two million dollars just doesn't seem fair," a small Japanese man spoke.

"I assure you, Mr. Lee, these top secret, military edition killing machines are worth the price tag. These aren't the kinds of weaponry you find in the waistbands of street thugs. These are war machines capable of mass destruction. One of these weapons in the hands of an American-hating piece of shit can do more damage at a state fair in one minute than five of those stupid-ass bombs they blew up at the Boston Marathon. The AX76 doesn't exist. A machine gun that fires explosives at five rounds a second is capable of mass destruction. And if your enemies have one and you don't?" Mr. Reign paused to look each man in the eyes.

A burly white man in a lavender suit spoke up. His name was Mr. Erickson. "When can we see them tested? What can they do?"

Mr. Reign gave a wicked smile. "They destroy. On impact, they explode. Microbits of C4 are inside the bullet. Our geniuses at the military R&R found out how to make the C4 inside the bullets explode when they hit a target."

The twelve men looked stunned. They were all perplexed by the destructive capability of C4-infused bullets, and they all knew if they didn't have one, or a crate, they wouldn't have the fire power to keep up with those who bought them.

Without including Mr. Reign, the twelve men turned to one another and began a heated, whispered discussion. A few minutes passed before they came to an agreement. Mr. Sanchez spoke. "We all agree the price of those machines are exorbitant, but in the wrong hands they could bring terror to our lives and ruin our collective futures. Here is our counter: 1.3 million per case, and you swat a fly that is nagging us. Not only will we take all the weapons you have, but we will also allow you a seat at the table with The Commission. We won't officially make you a member, but we will let you into the fold and give you a fair shake at becoming a member. This ain't a 'don't call us, we'll call you' thing. We are going to seriously consider letting you take an official seat, depending on how things go when we meet. The guys want to get a feel for you before getting into bed. You wouldn't just let a stranger into your family, would you? No matter that he dresses well or speaks eloquently. We're a family, Mr. Reign. We share a bond. One way in and one way out."

Mr. Reign nodded in approval. "I understand. Thank you for your time, gentleman, and I assure you a weapons testing will commence soon. I'll have twelve crates for you in 72 hours. Testing will be in two days, so make room on your busy schedules. Now, this fly that you need swatted. Tell me about it."

"Kasan Renaldi," Mr. Lee spoke.

A light of recognition went on in Mr. Reign's eyes.

"He got a bad rap from the feds, and we're concerned about the safety of The Commission. Something must be done. Erase his bloodline."

***

The four men dressed in black tactical suits and combat boots moved quickly and quietly, keeping their silenced automatic weapons high, moving with military precision towards the old factory. When they got as close as they could without being seen, the men took up positions, hiding in the darkness. The two-story building had been converted into a warehouse where million-dollar deals took place, and because of who was inside and what took place in the confines of its walls, the warehouse was under heavy guard.

Two men stood out front smoking, oblivious to the approaching danger.

Clap. Clap.

The complacent security guards fell to the ground, dropping their rifles, paying for their incompetence with bullets to the head. Without stopping to check the bodies, the team of trained killers moved toward the building.

When they got to the door, the lead man threw up a fist. After a series of hand signals, one of the men pulled several cylinder-shaped objects from his belt while another took a step back and kicked the door. As soon as the wood splintered, the man began lobbing the cylinders into the warehouse.

Voices shouted as the explosions began and the kill team rushed the building. Smoke from the flash-bang grenades and smoke bombs made it hard for the naked eye to see, but the killers didn't have that problem. They wore goggles that allowed them to see the heat signatures of the people in the room.

The silenced weapons clapped again, taking four more lives. When the bodies dropped to the floor, the team moved on, pausing outside a door at the back of the building. After a silent three count, the door was kicked off the hinges. On first glance, the room looked empty. The only things visible were caskets – ten rows stacked three high. The team moved toward the stack at the back of the room, surrounding it, weapons ready. Through the goggles they could see two heat signatures.

A frail man with skin the color of beach sand lay on the ground. The white t-shirt he wore was wrinkled, and his pants were around his ankles, showing red boxer briefs. Next to him was an attractive, pale-skinned woman in a blue dress.

"Who sent you? What do you want?" the man questioned, his Middle Eastern accent heavy.

No one on the kill team answered his question. Instead, one of the men pulled a radio from his waist. "Strong Man to Eagle. We have the package. Over."

A smooth voice responded. "Eagle to Strong Man. Secure the package. The Eagle has landed and has visitors. I'm coming in hot."

"Who are you? Whatever they're paying, I'll double it. No, I'll triple it! Just let me go. You can have it all," the man plead from the floor.

The kill team didn't speak, keeping their guns at the ready. A few moments later, Mr. Reign walked into the room carrying a duffel bag, floating like he was walking on air.

"Well, well, well. If it isn't the infamous Kasan Renaldi! And what do we have here? An unexpected guest? Side chick or woman of the night?"

Kasan stared up at the light-skinned man in confusion. "Wh-Who are you? How do you know my name? What do you want? Don't you know I'm connected? You will have to answer for this."

"Easy, fellas," Mr. Reign said, calling off his men. "And if I were you, Mr. Renaldi, I'd be more concerned about how the missus would feel if she found out you were running around with this pretty girl with your pants at your ankles."

Kasan's eyes grew wide with anger at the mention of his wife. "Who the hell do you think you are? What the fuck do you want?"

Mr. Reign laughed at the display of anger. "You're a fiery old man, huh? Well, I'll end the suspense. My name is Mr. Reign. I'm here to punish you for the deeds you did in the dark, which have come to the light."

Kasan was beside himself with anger. He jumped to his feet, pulled up his pants, and lunged for Mr. Reign. The kill team moved as one, pointing their weapons at the old man's chest. Kasan halted, staring at Mr. Reign with the fullness of his anger blazing in his eyes. "I don't know who you are, but I swear to Allah you will pay for this. I'm connected. You just put the lives of your entire family at risk. The Commission will avenge me."

"Speaking of family," Mr. Reign said, laying the duffle

bag on the coffin. After unzipping it, he began to unload an arsenal of weapons: a 12-gauge pump, .44 Magnum revolver, AK-47 with a folding bayonet, and a 50-caliber Desert Eagle. "Your actions have put the lives of your family members in my hand. Literally."

A commotion by the door got everyone's attention. A brown-skinned man wearing a wrinkled cream suit was escorted into the room at gunpoint. His hands were cuffed in front, duct tape covering his mouth. Shear terror was written all over his face.

When Kasan seen the kidnapped man, his demeanor went from angry to scared. "Please, don't do this. He doesn't know anything. He's the dean of a college. Leave him out of this."

"Right there is fine," Mr. Reign said, stopping the newcomer a few feet away. He picked up the .44 Magnum before turning back to Kasan. "What did you tell the feds?"

"Please, don't. My brother has nothing to do with this. I didn't tell the feds anything. I don't know what –"

Boom!

The .44 Magnum roared like thunder, sending a jolt through Mr. Reign's arm as it kicked back. A chunk of flesh and bone exploded from the dean's face as the slug hit home. The dead man fell backward, hitting the ground with a loud thud.

"No!" Kasan screamed. "You son of a bitch! I'm going to kill your whole family!"

"Make this easy on yourself, Kasan. Tell me what you told the feds. I know they came to see you."

"Fuck you! If you're going to kill me, do it. But you're going to pay for this. I swear on my son's life."

Mr. Reign dropped the revolver and picked up the shotgun. "Funny you should mention your son," he taunted before nodding to the man who brought in Kasan's brother.

The fear quickly returned to Kasan's eyes. "No! Please,

13

no. I'm sorry. I didn't mean it."

"Oh yeah!" Mr. Reign smiled, cocking the shotgun. A few moments later a ten-year-old boy and a woman who looked to be his mother were escorted into the room. Their hands were cuffed, and tape covered their mouths.

"Don't do this, Mr. Reign. Please. Leave my family out of this. It's me you want. Take me."

"Family, huh? Did you know I had a conversation with The Commission the other day, and they explained to me being part of that organization was like being family? Don't look so surprised. Yeah, they sent me. And I need that information. The lives of your family depend on it. What did you tell the feds?"

"Just let them go and I'll tell you everything. Please. They have nothing to do with this."

Boom!

The slug tore into the woman's chest, sending her body flying backward. Gurgling sounds came from her body as she struggled to breathe.

"No! Damn you, Reign! I'll kill you!" Kasan screamed, rushing Mr. Reign.

Clap.

"Ah!" Kasan screamed, falling to the ground and grabbing his wounded knee.

"This isn't a negotiation. Tell me what the fuck you told the feds!" Mr. Reign said, swapping the shotgun for the AK-47.

"Fuck you, Reign! And fuck The Commission! I told the feds everything. I named names. I gave them everything. I know how this ends. I know I'm going to die. Get it over with," Kasan grumbled in pain, trying to stand again.

Clap.

The bullet tore into his shin, snapping it in half. The old man's leg buckled, and he knew he would never stand again.

"You snitching-ass bitch," Mr. Reign said wickedly as he stood before Kasan's son with the chopper. With a deadly thrust, he shoved the bayonet blade into the boy's neck and squeezed the trigger. The boy's face exploded into pieces as the headless body fell to the ground.

Sobs wracked Kasan's body as he closed his eyes, awaiting his death. Mr. Reign swapped the AK-47 for the Desert Eagle and stood over Kasan. "I wish you could see what this bullet is about to do to you."

"Fuck you, you stupid –"

Boom!

Kasan's head exploded like a bomb was in his skull, sending blood and brains all over the room.

"Damn, that was messy," Mr. Reign frowned, wiping brain fragments from his suit. "Finish her off and clean this up. I have an important meeting I cannot miss."

Chapter 2

The line outside of *Cinco's* was a block long. Men and women in all manner of dress stood in the summer night air, waiting to be let into the five-story, state-of-the-art nightclub. The Glass House was on the first floor. It was a dance club made completely of glass. The second floor was The Foam Room, where the dance floor stayed covered in foam. Midnight was on the third floor. It was a gentleman's club that housed some of the sexiest women on the east coast. The Zone, a sports bar, was on the fourth floor. And on the rooftop was the five-star restaurant, Under the Moon.

Mr. Reign and the twelve men of The Commission were lounged around in Midnight, watching the performance on the stage. "Mr. Reign, your business venture is an amazing idea. I must admit I am a bit envious I didn't think of this," Mr. Obendowi said.

"Thank you. I invited you gentleman here to give you a glimpse into my business acumen and show you all I try to stay ahead of the curve when it comes to making power moves."

"I want to know if you are accepting investors?" Mr. Lee asked, taking his eyes off the women on stage. "A place like this has unlimited earning potential."

"Not at the moment. But if I garner the success I expect, I'll be looking to do businesses in other states and seeking investors. You'll be on my short list."

"Speaking of business," Mr. Sanchez spoke up. "The Commission wants to officially thank you for taking care of that fly for us. Were you able to glean any information about the investigation?"

"Unfortunately, no. The only thing I can confirm is that he was working with the feds, and he named names. But I have a few contacts who are working to uncover the details."

"You are proving to be a very valuable friend of The Commission," Steven McBride nodded. He was a black man from Atlanta who struck it rich in real estate. "If you can gather more information about the federal investigation, that would go a long way in securing your seat at the table."

"As I said, I will do what I can to help," Mr. Reign nodded.

The men turned their full attention back to the stage, watching two Asian women perform an X-rated show that would make one consider voting for erotic dancing as an Olympic event.

"Wow! That was a fine show," Vladimir Kundilovski, a tall, big-bearded Russian applauded. "Is there a place where we can see the performers up close and personal?"

Reign caught the meaning behind his words. "For you gentlemen, anything you want will be provided. There are rooms in the back. You may have your pick of any of the women, except the Japanese women, Sushi and Tushi."

***

"Thank you for inviting me, Mayor Christensen. The place looks...." Mr. Reign's words trailed off as he looked over the auditorium at the people who filled the seats. Just under two thousand men, women, and children were seated in the large room. Members of the media were also spread amongst the people, testing their equipment. "This is amazing," Mr. Reign continued. "It's hard to believe this building was a blueprint on your desk eighteen months ago."

Julian Christensen, the newly-elected mayor of New York, gave a winning smile as he sat a plump, tanned hand on the shoulder of Mr. Reign's tailored black suit. "None of this would be possible without your help. Your donations to my campaign and the charities is what brought this to life.

This is a result of your work, as well. This center will change the lives of so many people and will be worth the 1.8 million dollar price tag."

Mr. Reign extended a large hand, grasping the mayor's and pulling him in for a bear hug. The media jumped at the unexpected display of affection and cameras flashed as the crowd applauded the display of brotherly love.

"This means more to me than you know," Mr. Reign said after loosening the embrace.

"How about you send me a card or gift the next time you want to show your gratitude?" The mayor grimaced, stretching his back and rolling his neck. "Your hugs are lethal, man. Lay off the weights."

Reign laughed. "Sorry about that."

After a few more back bends, Julian Christensen walked toward the microphone. "Is this thing on? Testing." Upon hearing his voice, the crowd simmered down and gave him their attention. And being the good politician he was, the mayor took it all in. His gray eyes began to water, and he wore an awestruck look on his chubby face as he spanned the room.

"Wow! Isn't this awesome? Black, white, young, old, police, civilian, business people, and politicians from both sides. This is what America looks like. Citizens gathered for the greater good of us all." A thunderous applause went up front the audience, causing the mayor to pause. "Ladies and gentlemen, boys and girls, we are all gathered in this place for a great cause. The grand opening of the Calvin Acosta Center is a monumental occasion, and this is a great day for the city of New York. The reason we brought the center to this neighborhood is because you deserve and need it. The jobless rates, poverty rates, and incarceration rates are astounding, and as the newly-elected mayor I promised I would bring opportunity and problem solving to everyone who needs it. This center is a down payment on that promise. It is not a cure-all, but the beginning of finding that cure. And rest assured I will not rest until all the men, women, and children in this community have the same opportunities as those in the well-off places in this nation. I want you to know none of this would be possible if it wasn't for the help of the man standing behind me. His philanthropic donations were God-sent. Without further ado, allow me to introduce Mr. Reign!"

The ovation that went up from the people rivaled that of fans cheering at a sports event. Mr. Reign paused at the microphone, taking in a little more adoration before lifting his arms and calming them.

"Thank you so much for that warm welcome. I am humbled and honored to stand before you today. As some of you know, I grew up in this neighborhood so being able to give back the place that made me is a wonderful thing. And like the mayor said, we won't stop here. I am standing before you because I got the opportunity to make a way for myself. That's what many of you need. Not help, but opportunity. And this center will provide that. Take advantage of these resources.

"This is more than just a building to me. A few months ago my brother was a victim...." Mr. Reign paused, clenching his jaw as he fought back tears. The crowd waited on edge as he gathered himself. "My brother, Calvin Acosta, was killed because of senseless violence. As a tribute to him and my desire to stop as many senseless killings as I can, I got behind the mayor's plans to help our community. Minority violence is an epidemic. Something must be done. Prisons and graveyards are filled with men and women who, if given the opportunity, would've made something of their lives. It is my hope that this center will be a catalyst of opportunity for everyone."

***

"So, how did I do?" Mr. Reign asked as he relaxed in the plush, leather back seat of the Cadillac Escalade.

"They ate up every fucking word. Denzel ain't got shit on you," Virgil laughed from the passenger seat. The dark-skinned, bald Haitian man was one of Mr. Reign's personal bodyguards.

"I don't really like the spotlight, but this was important. Jackson's bitch-ass is getting on my nerves, and I need a powerful ally. Hopefully my connection to the mayor will keep his punk-ass at bay. If not…."

"I like 'if not,'" Virgil smiled.

Reign laughed. "You would, you sick-ass nigga. Jackson needs to die, but not right now. Can't get sloppy when you kill a fed."

"Just say when and it's done."

The Cadillac rode smoothly through the busy New York traffic, seemingly disappearing amongst the congestion. None of the occupants noticed the black sedan trailing a half block away until the lights began flashing.

"We got company," Banks, the Escalade driver, announced.

Mr. Reign spun around to look out the back window. The black sedan with flashing lights closed quickly on the SUV's bumper. "Bitch-ass nigga."

"You want me to take care of that?" Virgil asked, reaching for the .45 in his shoulder holster.

"Nah. A pest can't be killed like this. This will take patience. Pull over, Banks."

Agent Marshall Jackson moved with the grace of a big cat as he walked toward the black luxury vehicle. He wasn't a big man, only five ten with a lean build, but his presence filled any room he walked into.

The look on his face was stone, but on the inside he

giggled. There were only a few things he loved more than making bad guys uncomfortable. After stopping at the tinted back window, he gave it a tap. When it rolled down, he could see the blazing hatred in Mr. Reign's eyes. And he loved it.

"How are you today, Mr. Reign?"

His face remained neutral while discontentment showed in his eyes. "Quit the bullshit, Jackson. What do you want? I have important business to handle."

"Why the hostilities? I come in peace, to talk friend-to-friend."

"None of my friends wear badges."

Jackson's laugh was hearty. "I beg to differ. You've corrupted some of New York's finest. I've seen the Internal Affairs reports. Your name bleeds from the pages. You befriended those cops, so why can't we be friends?"

"Because your self-righteousness is nauseating. Your voice is irritating. And you stink. Like pork. I don't eat swine."

The laughter quickly faded from Jackson's features. "I heard the press conference with the mayor. Do you think rubbing elbows with politicians and some bullshit philanthropy will keep me from busting your ass? Think again, Reign. I'm onto you. I know you're dirty. I know you're a scumbag. And when a judge sentences your ass to life in federal prison, I'm going to have the last laugh."

Mr. Reign looked un-phased by the threats. "I'll tell the mayor you said 'hi'. Now, if you're done harassing me, I'd like to be on my way. I have business to tend. If you want to talk again, call my lawyer. You have the number."

The look on the federal agent's face spoke of his anger. He wanted Mr. Reign in chains, locked in a cell, just as bad as he wanted to take his next breath.

No more words were exchanged between the men. Only cold, hard stares.

"Let's go, Banks," Mr. Reign said, tapping the driver's seat. "It was nice seeing you again, Agent Jackson."

J-Blunt

Chapter 3

"What time does the shipment of guns arrive?" Mr. Reign asked, sloshing cognac around the glass before taking a drink.

He was in the back office at Midnight. The man he was speaking with was Santos, a Mexican in his early forties who loved tequila and gambling as much as breathing. He was a small man with a slim build and shiny black hair pulled into a ponytail. They had been business partners for almost two years, though none of their deals were as big as the one with The Commission.

"A day. Maybe two. Customs has been giving our transports a hard time. America's war on immigration is affecting us all."

Mr. Reign gave the slim, greasy-haired man a displeased look. "I can't wait 'til tomorrow. Those guns were supposed to be here today. You said so a week ago. Important people are waiting for those crates. I need them now! Not later. Now!"

A slight tremble vibrated through the little man's body. "It is out of our hands, Reign. I cannot speed up a ship. I don't even know where the ship is at the moment. As I've said, progress has been stalled."

A crease spread through Mr. Reign's forehead as he frowned. "What do you mean you don't know where the ship is? Those crates are worth millions of dollars!"

Santos shifted nervously, uneasy about making the boss angry. "Um, well, sir, there has been a lapse in communication. But I assure you my people are doing everything they can to reestablish communication."

"And you're just now telling me about this lapse in communication? How long have you known?"

"Uh. Since yesterday."

Mr. Reign let out a long sigh before draining the liquor

from the glass. The temperature in the room rose noticeably, making those present shift nervously. Instead of yelling to express his anger, Mr. Reign's spoke softly. "Why wasn't I notified of the delay?"

"I didn't want to burden you with the particulars. It is just a slight lapse in time. I'm handling things. The guns will be here tomorrow."

"Do you believe in keeping your word, Santos?" Mr. Reign asked, eyeing the Latin man as he reclined in the chair.

"Always. Our word is our bond."

"I gave my word to twelve of the most powerful men in the world that I would have those guns this evening. Now I will have to go back on my word. How do you think that will make me look in their eyes?"

Santos adjusted the collar on his shirt. "Um, I'm not sure I can answer that, sir. I don't want to place myself in your shoes. They are too big to fill."

A sinister smile spread across Mr. Reign's face. "Your flattery is unwelcome. Now, answer the question."

Santos paused to think. "It could be a setback. Powerful men expect actions, not excuses."

"So, you see my problem?"

"Yes. I do."

"Tonight there will be a weapons testing. I will send someone to pick you up. The men I'm meeting with want to see what the weapons can do. I'll also need you to explain to them why their purchases will be late. That is all."

Santos and his assistant left the room quickly.

"Should I kill him?" Virgil asked.

Reign looked irritated. "No. Why would you say that?"

"Because I know you don't tolerate failure." He paused. "And I also don't like him. I think he's a snake."

Mr. Reign laughed. "If you killed everybody you didn't like, New York would be missing half its population. Relax.

Everything will occur when it's supposed to. Do you have any news on who killed my brother?"

"We have a couple of leads we're looking into. A pimp named Las Vegas or Garcia Vega is supposed to know something. I have some guys tracking him down. They will call me when they know something."

"Good. Good. I knew Calico would get himself killed eventually. He was the smartest fool I ever knew. Someone has to pay for this."

"How do you know he's dead? What if he's still alive? They still haven't found his body."

"Because I know. It's been almost two months since anyone's seen or heard from him. That's not like my brother. He's flashy, wants everybody to know he's important. He's dead. I know it. And I want to find out who did it and make them pay for it. They will suffer like my family has suffered."

***

Expectant energy flowed through the airplane hangar in waves, causing the twelve men present to constantly fidget in their seat. Champagne and appetizers were spread out on the table before them, but none of them indulged much. Anticipation of the show culled their desires for food and drink.

"Where is he? We have been here for twenty minutes. Does he dare insult The Commission?" Mr. Obendowi breathed.

"Perhaps this is a set-up, huh? Have we vetted him to the fullest extent?" Mr. Lee asked.

"Relax, gentleman," Mr. Sanchez spoke. "He has been fully vetted. This is all a part of his show. He's making us stir. It's called gamesmanship, my friends. He will –"

The hangar doors opening forced Mr. Sanchez to stop

talking. The Commission watched as the black luxury SUV drove slowly into the airplane hangar. When the doors opened, three men exited the vehicle. Santos, Virgil, and Mr. Reign took up the rear, carrying a black briefcase.

"My apologies for the delay, gentlemen," Mr. Reign spoke. "I was fine tuning some last minute developments, but now we will proceed with the testing. In this briefcase is the AX76, and I will demonstrate its destructive power without further ado. My bodyguard will be my second. Virgil, proceed."

The Haitian popped the trunk of the Escalade and began unloading a number of items. A tree trunk. A watermelon. A bulletproof fiberglass window. And a car door. While Virgil set up the props, Mr. Reign showed off the weapon. It was black as death, 36 inches from front to back with a six-inch barrel and a twelve-inch folding stock. There was a lever on the side that switched the firing from a semi automatic, three-round burst to fully automatic. A 25-round clip filled with thirty caliber explosive bullets hung from the bottom. Upon first look, most people thought it was a space gun.

"The hardware looks nice. Shall we get on with the demonstration?" Mr. Lee questioned.

Mr. Reign nodded. "As you wish."

Virgil set the props a hundred feet from where Mr. Reign stood. He began with the watermelon. After setting the firing lever on semi, he gave the trigger a squeeze. The watermelon exploded, sending slush and juice spraying everywhere. The tree trunk was next. A single shot ripped a chunk from the trunk the size of a basketball, setting a small fire around the crater and sending the rest flying across the hanger. A second shot pulverized the trunk into wood chips. Next was the bulletproof fiberglass. Mr. Reign set the firing switch on burst and squeezed the trigger. Three rounds slapped into the glass, chipping it as they exploded. Another volley shattered the bulletproof glass, leaving the members of the commission astonished. For the finale, he turned the gun upon the car door. After switching the AX76 to fully automatic, he squeezed and held the trigger. The gun erupted, sounding like it was firing tank rounds as the car door was blown apart. The Commission stood and applauded.

"My God!" Mr. Obendowi exclaimed. "That weapon is devil spawned! And I love it."

Mr. Lee's eyes were wide with awe. "Not even bulletproof glass can stop the rounds!"

"Fuck the glass. Did you see what it did to that door?" Mr. Sanchez spoke, lust in his eyes.

"Where are my guns?" Steven McBride asked eagerly.

Mr. Reign turned his gaze upon Santos. "Gentlemen of The Commission, this is the man in charge of bringing your weapons across the seas. Aladan Santos. Mr. Santos, why don't you explain to these men the whereabouts of their precious cargo."

The brown-skinned man blanched under the intense stares of the powerful men. "Sure. Um. There has been a slight delay. Customs is causing the freight some issues. We should have the guns tomorrow."

"Should?" Mr. Sanchez inquired, raising an eyebrow.

"Yes. Should. You see, there has been a lapse in communication with the ship."

"What is he talking about, Mr. Reign?" Mr. Obendowi roared, the frustration showing in his eyes.

"He just spoke of his incompetence, sirs. As things are right now, he doesn't know where the guns are."

Gasps went up from The Commission. "And what is being done about this?" Vladimir Kundilovski asked.

"Ev-everything, sir. I have men working on establishing communication with the ship."

"This is not good." Mr. Sanchez breathed.

"If there is anything I can do to please you, let me know," Santos pled.

"The only thing you can do is get my damn guns!" Mr. Lee yelled.

"As I've told you, we're working on it."

"Gentlemen, let me apologize for the delay," Mr. Reign spoke. "Unfortunately, I have aligned myself with a man who does not share my beliefs about keeping one's word and the need for transparency. As a result, if it pleases the Commission, Mr. Santos has given his body as a test prop to show the AX76's destructive power on a human subject."

A few members of The Commission nodded.

Santos turned white with fear, holding his hands up and backing away. "N-no! Please, don't do this! This is just a small setback. I know I fucked up, but I will make it right. Please!"

The bullet exploded into the right side of Santos' chest, blowing his entire arm from the shoulder socket. Santos was lifted off his feet, his body twisting in the air, landing on the ground a few feet away. His arm flew in the opposite direction. Blood poured from his shoulder wound, the pain so excruciating he couldn't scream. His eyes were bucked, mouth wide open, but no sound came out. Reign aimed the gun at his face and fired another bullet. There was a small explosion as Santos' head evaporated. His body twitched for a few moments before all movement ceased.

"Gentlemen, I assure you I will do everything possible to correct this fool's mistake. You will have your purchases soon."

Mr. Obendowi gave Mr. Reign a long look. "Your seat at the table is depending on it."

After assuring The Commission he would get their guns, all parties left the airplane hanger. Mr. Reign sat down and poured himself a drink. "Virgil, call someone to clean up this mess."

"You got it, boss," the Haitian said, pulling out his phone. Before he could dial a number, it rang. "Hello? Mr. Reign, it is for you."

"This is Reign," he spoke before pausing to listen. The frown of his eyebrows and curling of his top lip reflected his emotions. "Who the fuck is Syn?"

J-Blunt

Chapter 4

Syn

I had killed before for many reason. Mostly self preservation. Somewhere in my mind I justified that what I did had to be done. It was either me or them. No matter who's blood or how much got spilled, those justifying words helped ease my conscious and allowed me to sleep peacefully every night.

All of that was before I killed my daughter.

Father will be divided against son, and son against father, mother against daughter, and daughter against mother.

Somehow that scripture jumped out of the Bible and lodged itself in my brain. I don't remember reading it or hearing it spoken. I can't even remember the last time I went to church. It had been years. All I know is the verse popped into my head one day, and now I can't stop thinking about it. Is God trying to tell me something? Am I marked for death? Have evil deeds polluted my soul so much that Bible verses popped into my mind without me knowing how they got there? And why hadn't any more verses come? Why just this one?

I'm sorry, Trinity. I miss you so much.

A knock on the door pulled me from the dark thoughts. "Come in."

When the office door opened, my assistant, Derikka, peeked inside. "Mrs. Brookshire just canceled the one o'clock meeting. She said something about a prior engagement that couldn't wait. She wants to reschedule next Monday. Same time."

As I watched her lips form the words, I couldn't help but think of how much my assistant reminded me of Trinity. Similar thick and curly hair. Same light-skinned complexion. Even her height and physical build was the same. She was

33

young, pretty, energetic, and full of life. The darkness in the world hadn't polluted her soul, so she remained optimistic about everything. I wondered somewhere in the back of my mind if I hired her because she looked like my daughter.

"Did you hear me, Syn?" she asked.

"Yeah. I heard you," I managed, snapping out of my zone. "I'm fine with the reschedule. That was my last meeting for the day, right?"

She looked down at her phone, checking my schedule. "Yeah. I just need you to look over a couple contracts."

"Okay. Thank you."

Instead of leaving, Derikka lingered in my doorway like she had more to say.

"Do you need anything else?"

"Um. No. Not really. I just wanted to know if you were okay. I know Trinity –"

"You can leave now," I cut her off. I didn't mean to be mean or rude, but she needed to know we were not coworkers or friends. I was her boss, and she couldn't ask personal questions about my life.

"Uh. Okay. Sorry," she apologized before leaving my office.

I closed my eyes and reclined in the chair, taking a deep breath and letting it out slowly. I had been looking forward to that appointment with Debra Brookshire. She had connections to Victoria's Secret and the Sports Illustrated Magazine Swimsuit Issue. If I could get in bed with one of those companies, the sky was the limit for Synful Desires. Plus, I needed to keep myself busy. Idle time played tricks on my mind, so I overindulged myself with work. And sex.

Luke said I had become a workaholic to cope with losing Trinity, and he might've had a point. Work and sex were the only things that kept my mind off murdering my daughter. And the pills. After finding my purse, I grabbed the bottle of

Oxycontin and popped two, chasing them with a sip of bottled water. Then my phone rang. Tahiti's picture popped up on the screen.

"Hey, baby," I smiled. Seeing her face removed some of the melancholy from my mood.

"Hey, girl. What you up to?"

"Nothing. The Brookshire bitch just canceled our one o'clock meeting. Ugly white bitch."

Tahiti giggled. "Why her old ass playing them games? Don't she know we trying to make power moves."

"I know, right?" I agreed. "Victoria's Secret runway needs one of my girls. Show the whole world how much of a boss Syncere Evans is. Put Synful Desires on the map. But the old bitch got plans she can't break, so we rescheduled."

"Well, better luck next time. And just in case you need a real woman to hit that runway and show them skinny bitches how to slay in some lingerie and angel wings, I'm your girl."

"Now, that's funny!" I laughed. "You got way too much ass and titties for them. Plus, Luke needs you. Speaking of my husband, where is he?"

Tahiti let out a heavy sigh. "Him and Travis in a meeting. I swear they been in there for an hour. What could possibly be that important that they have to talk for so long?"

"Don't sound like you feeling this secretary thing?"

"I'm a receptionist. Get it right," Tahiti corrected. "And I hate this shit. It's so boring. I sit at a desk and answer the phone and run errands. Y'all lucky I love y'all asses, or I swear I would've quit."

"It ain't that bad," I laughed. "Plus, they need you. They are starting an accounting firm from the bottom. Stick with it. It will get better."

"Yeah, I know. I wish you could at least be here with me. You want to meet for lunch? I have a break in fifteen minutes."

I thought for moment. "You know what? I'm on my way over. I'm done over here for the day. I'ma see you in a few minutes."

After a few words with Derikka, I left the modeling agency, flexing in a colorful Salvatore Ferragamo top, white Esteban Cortazar pants, and black Ferragamo heels. After hopping in my lime green Porsche 911 GT3 RS, I drove for twenty minutes before parking in front of a building seemingly made of glass. Glass double doors and floor-to-ceiling glass windows covered the front of the building. "Swanson & Kratz" was stenciled across the windows in big, block letters. Tahiti sat behind the desk wearing a plain black skirt suit, looking bored and uninterested.

"You have to smile to bring up the energy and morale," I cracked.

Tahiti gave me sharp look before blinking away the boredom and putting on her best smile. "Welcome to Swanson & Kratz. I'm Tahiti Johnson. How may I assist you today?"

"That's more like it," I applauded before leaning across the desk to peck her on the lips. "Where are the money men, anyway?"

"In the conference room, still having that boring-ass meeting," she sulked, pointing to the smoked windows toward the back of the building.

The windows could be lightened or darkened by knobs on the inside and outside of the room. I had an idea. "C'mon, Tahiti."

"He doesn't want to be bothered unless it's an emergency."

I waved her words off and continued toward the conference room. "Quit being scared. C'mon."

I stopped at the window tinting knobs and waited for my girl. Mischief and fear shown in her eyes as she approached.

36

I wrapped an arm around her waist, pulling her close as I reached for the knob. Right before our lips locked, I twisted the knob. Our hands roamed one another's body as our tongues danced. Out of the corner of my eyes, I watched the reactions from the people in the room. Two white men and a black woman looked shocked. Then, slowly, their looks changed to amusement and then interest. Travis Kratz looked turned on. And Luke looked pissed off. He gave us an angry stare, and I could only imagine the angry thoughts running through his mind. After we finished making out, I blew Luke a kiss before twisting the tinting knob and leaving.

"He is going to kill us," Tahiti giggled as we hopped in my Porsche.

"He'll be okay. Make sure you text him and let him know you're with me, and we'll be out for lunch."

"I did. And I'm not hungry. My appetite has been crazy lately."

I glanced over at her. She was filling out that skirt suit in ways that would make an insecure woman not want to stand next to her. Her titties were sitting up in the blouse like she had balloons under her shirt. Her ass and thighs were thick and shapely. And to top it all off, my girl was fine with long, black hair, beautiful brown skin, full lips, and dimples in her cheeks. She reminded me of Nikki Minaj.

"Looks like you've been eating good to me. Your ass looks phatter than ever."

"I know. I feel fat."

"Girl, stop. Didn't you just talk about walking runways and showing the world what a real woman looks like?"

"I did, didn't I?" she laughed. "I'm a woman, so I'm allowed to change my mind."

"Stop stealing my lines, nigga. I know you heard me tell Luke that yesterday."

"Maybe I did. But I make it sound better. I got that drip."

I rolled my eyes. "Whatever. Since you don't want to eat, run to the Michael Kors store with me. I seen a dress I wanted."

"Now, that's what I'm talking about. My ass could use a new skirt."

When we got to the store, we browsed around a little before making our selections and hitting the changing room. I was trying on a purple dress while Tahiti struggled to get into a pair of white pants. Her titties jiggled wildly, threatening to spill from her bra, as she jumped up and down, trying to shimmy into the fabric.

"Why not get a bigger size?"

"I did," she grunted. "These are a twelve."

"Damn. I knew you looked a little thicker," I said, looking her over when she finally got the pants on. Her ass looked amazing in the white denim.

"What do you think?" she asked, twirling to check her angles in the mirror. My feelings for Tahiti had grown by leaps and bounds since Luke came home and we all moved in together. I was in love with both of them. Luke more, but as I stared at Tahiti's sexy ass, my pussy got wet.

"I think your ass looks good enough to take a bite out of," I said before slapping her cheeks and watching them jiggle.

"My thighs is rubbing. I need to go on a diet," she whined.

While Tahiti complained, I checked out my figure in the dress. It fit me perfectly. I couldn't wait 'til Luke seen me in this. "How do I look?" I asked, twirling for my girl.

"Like a fine-ass grape," she cracked, trying to get the pants off. Her breasts and jiggly parts bounced around again. It made me want to fuck.

"Sit down and let me help you take them off."

When she sat down, I got on my knees and helped her get the pants off. When she tried to stand again, I wasn't having it. "Stay right there. Let me look at you."

She read my mind and lay back in the chair, giving sexy expressions while rubbing her body. "You like what you see?"

My girl looked like a perfect ten sitting in the chair. I grabbed her foot and began kissing my way up her leg. She let out the sexiest moans that got my pussy even wetter. When I got to her inner thighs, I paused to take off her panties. Tahiti's pussy was beautiful, the same skin tone as the rest of her body and meaty. No hair. Her labia was swollen and slick with her sweet juices. I loved tasting that sweet juice when I sucked her pussy after Luke fucked her.

After tossing her panties aside, I dove in, licking and sucking her love button. When she was on the verge of cumming, I reached up and freed her titties from her bra. Her nipples were hard as rocks. When I squeezed them, instead of loving it, she grabbed my hand and held it.

"No, Syn. My nipples hurt."

I didn't give her words much thought. I was too focused on making her cum so she could return the favor. So, instead of teasing her breasts, I began fingering her while sucking her clit. When she grabbed fistfuls of my hair, I knew she was about to cum. Then her body went stiff and she let out a low moan. I kept drinking her juices until her orgasm passed.

Seeing, feeling, and tasting her orgasm had me dripping. I jumped up and snatched the dress over my head. Tahiti was upon me before I could get her dress off. She pushed me against the wall and shoved her tongue down my throat, tasting her own juices. Then she dropped to her knees and started eating me.

I turned my head, watching in the mirror as she sucked my pussy. Seeing her on her knees while I stood over her made me feel powerful, how I imagined Luke felt when I was on my knees giving him head. When her fingers slipped into my pussy, I closed my eyes and tilted my head back. The pills had taken effect, and I was riding a perfect high. It felt like I was in my own world.

My moans got louder as the orgasm approached. By the time I came, I was screaming way too loud to be in a high-end fashion changing room.

"Hey! What's going on in here?" a woman called.

For some reason I thought the situation was funny and started laughing. Tahiti looked scared, her eyes wide as full moons. "Um. We're on our way out. We, uh."

"We got stuck," I laughed. "Here we come."

"Hurry up! This is a place of business, not a porno set."

"Damn, Syn. That shit ain't funny. Let's get the fuck out of here before they call the police," Tahiti said, getting dressed quickly.

"You shouldn't be so good at eating pussy."

After paying for our things and getting lustful looks from the security guard, we hopped in my car and headed back to the accounting firm.

"What's wrong with your breasts? Why are they sore?" I asked.

"I'm not sure. My nipples are tender and aching. And I'm gaining weight and feeling nauseous all the time."

Even though I was high, I immediately knew what was going on, and that shit got me angrier by the moment. I took my eyes off the road to look at her reaction. "Have you taken a pregnancy test?"

She looked surprised by the question. "What? Why?"

"Because it sounds like you're pregnant. Have you taken a test?"

She let out a nervous laugh. "Girl, you tripping. Ain't nobody pregnant."

"I think you are. We're stopping at the store to get you a test."

"Syn, that ain't necessary. I'm good."

I mugged her ass, stopping the argument before it started. "This is not up for discussion. We're going to get you a test."

J-Blunt

Chapter 5

Luke

"Damn, Luke! I can't believe we did it!" Travis smiled, shaking his head from side to side, elation and relief plastered on his face. "We just got Milton Braggard's accounts, brah. The owner of Nebula Force wants us to play with his purse!"

Travis was my boy from way back. He took me under his wing and helped me out when I first started at Marty and Sloan's Accounting Firm after I graduated college. He was thirty-four years old, and stood about six-six with a slim build and light skin. He reminded me of a tall Terence Howard.

"I told you we could do it, brother." I grabbed a flute of champagne from the table, holding it in the air. "We're too talented and too smart not to be successful. And I been through so much over the past two years that I needed a win. For a minute I thought God bailed on me."

Travis grabbed a flute and clinked it against my glass. "This toast is for Milton Braggard and his one hundred million dollars. And for your freedom. Glad you're back in the free world, brother."

We took drinks of the bubbly, celebrating the catch of our first big fish at our brand spanking new accounting firm. I had come up with the plans while I was locked up, and with Syn being a millionaire, I knew I had to get out and pull my own weight. Starting a new firm in a new city was risky, but once I convinced Travis we could do it, he left Sachs and got on board. And now it was done. Two brothers out of the hood heading their own accounting firm and landing a hundred million dollar client in the first three months was an accomplishment worth celebrating.

"I gotta be honest, man, I was super skeptical about leaving Sachs. This was a leap for me, to turn down a six-figure salary for a dream I never had. But I'm glad as hell I did. Woo!"

"Only way to be successful is to take a leap of faith." I took a sip from the glass of bubbly and looked out the conference room window. Syn had just walked into the firm with Tahiti, and they were headed in our direction. I was happy to see them, too. I couldn't wait to celebrate with my girls. But first I was going to get in their asses for the shit they pulled, making out in front of Milton and his lawyers.

"I know y'all thought that shit was funny. And if y'all wasn't so fine and we didn't get this client, I would've been pissed off."

Instead of getting smiles and compliments from my ladies, I got angry eyes from Syn and sadness from Tahiti. "How long have you known Tahiti was pregnant?" Syn demanded.

I looked at Tahiti, hoping to get a read from her expression on how much Syn knew and how to proceed. My pregnant girlfriend could only close her eyes and take a deep breath, looking like she wanted to wish herself away from the confrontation.

"Why are you looking at her? I'm the one talking to you," Syn continued, getting angrier by the moment.

I set the glass of champagne on the table and reached out to her. "Relax, baby. I wa–"

She slapped my hands away. "Don't touch me, nigga! Fuck you mean, 'relax'? Tahiti is pregnant! How long have you known?"

"I think I'm going to step out," Travis said, grabbing his suit jacket.

"Did you know, Travis?" Syn accused before turning her anger back at me. "Did you tell him before you told me?"

"I don't know what the hell you're talking about, Syncere. And this don't have nothing to do with me. I'm leaving. Luke, we still have to catch that flight. Call me when you're on the way to the airport."

"I was going to tell you, baby, but I didn't know how. I knew this wasn't part of the plan."

"How about just telling me?" Syn asked. "Tahiti missed per period three months ago! And why the fuck is Travis talking about catching a plane?"

"We have to fly to Washington to meet with a potential client. It just came up. And I'm sorry for not telling you sooner. I was going to tell you. Shit was just complicated."

Her eyes grew so wide I thought they would pop out of her head. "When were you going to tell me, Luke? After the baby popped out? I swear, I should beat both y'all asses for playing with me like this. You know I can't have kids, and I just lost…." She stopped snapping to blink away the tears and stop her lip from quivering.

Seeing my girl hurting made me hurt. She hadn't talked much about killing Trinity, but I knew it was fucking with her. She had become a heavy drinker to cope, and hearing Tahiti was having my baby was the nail in the coffin.

"We wasn't playing with you, baby," Tahiti spoke up. "I was taking birth control. I didn't want to get pregnant. I love you."

Slap!

Tahiti stumbled backward, almost losing her balance.

"Shut the fuck up, bitch!" Syn exploded. "I don't want to hear that shit. I'm talking to my man. Stay out of this. If you loved me, you would've told me. We had an arrangement. Both of y'all played me."

While Tahiti rubbed her stinging face, I intervened. "Hitting her won't solve nothing. We can't change her being pregnant. She's having our baby. But that doesn't mean we have to let this break us apart. Tahiti is our girlfriend. She lives with us. She sleeps with us. She works with us."

Syn looked like she wanted to attack me. "Oh, so y'all supposed to be a family now?"

"Now that she is pregnant, yes, she is our family. This can make us stronger. We can raise the baby together. It might be able to fill the hole Trinity left."

"Motherfucker!" she screamed, taking a wild swing at me that I wasn't able to dodge. "Don't talk about her baby and my daughter! This is not about us being a family. This is about y'all lying and stabbing me in the back. You know how I feel about you. I stood by your ass while you were locked up. I made sure you lived like a boss while you was locked up. Had pussy and cell phones. We are supposed to be best friends that tell each other everything."

I felt even worse when she recapped her loyalty to me while I was locked up, but she had been dishonest, too, and I wasn't about to let her lay all the guilt on me. "You got some responsibility in this, too, Syn. Don't act like this is all my fault. I went to jail and risked my life protecting your ass. You the one that started off lying to me about all kinds of shit. Calico. The money. Shit, I didn't even know your real name 'til after we started getting shot at. Only reason I started fucking her was because of you. You brought her to us. I'm sorry we didn't tell you right away. We should've. As your man, I should've. But this where we at now."

Tears ran down her face and she stared at me like she wanted to go toe-to-toe. "You know what? Fuck both of y'all. Go ahead and be a family and raise y'all baby," she cursed before turning and walking away.

I wanted to stop her from leaving, but that would've been a bad idea. She was feeling violent and needed time. As much as I wanted to grab her by the arm and make her stay until we worked it out, I knew I had to let her go. It was best for all of us.

"What do you want me to do?" Tahiti asked, sorrow in

her eyes.

I ran a hand across my face and let out a long breath. "Nothing you can do. Just leave her alone. I'll talk to her when I get back. I have to catch a flight in a couple of hours."

She looked incredulous. "You're still leaving? We need to fix this first."

"You know how Syn is. She doesn't want to talk right now. There is nothing we can do. And this company is important to our future. Missing a meeting with a client won't solve our issue. We have to let her deal with this in her own way. Don't go home tonight. Sleep in a hotel until I get back."

She looked like she wanted to cry. "I don't want to be here without you. Syn is crazy. Can I come with you?"

"Nah, that might not be a good idea. If Syn finds out you went out of town with me, she will swear we're sneaking around behind her back. Get a hotel. I should be back tomorrow. Maybe the next day. I'll call you later, baby."

***

A round of turbulence rocked The 747's business class. The plane vibrated and everything around me shook for a few seconds. It was a normal part of flying, so I wasn't too concerned about the shakes. What occupied most of my thoughts were my women. Damn. It was all good just a couple hours ago. Last night I was sandwiched between two dimes, getting double the pleasure and double the fun with thoughts of being a millionaire playing in my head. Now my perfect flight in life had also hit a patch of turbulence. I knew I would work it out eventually, but it didn't help that I would have this on my mind before an important meeting. Another million-dollar client would add to our success and establish our reputation as businessmen.

"Where your head at?" Travis asked. "You're not going

to let home get in the way of business, right? Gotta get this money, brotha."

"C'mon, Trav. I perform my best under pressure. You know that. We're getting Harmon's account, just like I got the owner of Jasmine Cosmetics to join at Marty and Sloan's."

He gave a long, searching look. "Okay. My bad. I forgot Luke Swanson is clutch. Been a couple years since we worked together, and I forgot what it was like to work someone I can trust."

"That's right. Respect the crown," I laughed halfheartedly.

"You got it, king. So, why didn't you tell nobody Tahiti was pregnant? You knew she would find out eventually. You can't hide a baby."

"We wasn't trying to hide it. I was going to tell her. But Syn ain't the kind of woman that takes bad news well."

He laughed. "So you was scared to tell her?"

"Hell nah. Fuck you, nigga. I run my shit. I'm good. I was going to tell her. Everything been so fucked up around us that I wanted to wait 'til we got some good news first. But I'm good. Syn is not going anywhere. Trust me."

"You still should've told her. I thought you had it good with two girlfriends, but now that I see the kind of problems they can cause, I'm going to stay a one-woman man."

That made me laugh. "You're not a one-at-a-time kinda nigga. You get caught up, too. I remember the shit that went down with Destiny. She fucked up the Audi."

"Okay. You got me right there," he admitted after a chuckle. "Man, I loved that car. You think Syn will fuck up some of your shit while we're out of town?"

I gave it some thought. "Nah. That ain't Syn. She would probably shoot me before it came to that."

Travis's stare got serious, eyes popping. "Syncere is shoot-a-nigga crazy?"

The situation wasn't funny, but his reaction was. "I think Syn will put in work if she needs to."

"Damn, li'l brah. I never thought her to be that type. I knew she was headstrong, but I didn't know you had a Cookie Lyons. She would cut your dick off while you sleep. Have you waking up screaming and blood coming out that hole where your dick used to be."

"C'mon, man. Don't put that energy in the atmosphere. We good."

"Y'all might be made for each other. You and Barron have shown me Swansons go hard. You have a hell of a story to tell. Should write a book about it. You went from a prison cell to a million-dollar firm. That's a best seller."

"No books in my future. I'm sticking to the stock. Pays more."

"Serious question. With everything you've been through in the last two years – prison, killing someone, and getting shot – if you could do everything over, would you do it again?"

I took a few moments to think on my response. "Honestly, I wouldn't change a thing. Everything I went through made me everything I am. I wouldn't recommend my path for nobody, but I learned a lot about myself. Facing death, killing a man, and a prison cell taught me a lot about who I am. It all made me stronger."

Travis nodded. "That was real shit. I mean, I definitely wouldn't have responded the same way if I had spent two years in prison, got shot, and killed someone. I would do all that shit over. Fuck that. But I get it. That whole knowledge-of-self concept is a good thing to have. Best way to find out if you like men is to shower with them everyday," he laughed.

I mugged him. "Fuck you, nigga. They didn't have community showers in the prisons I was in. Plus, yo' soft ass wouldn't have made it in Waupun. You would be following

your man across the yard holding his belt loop."
He didn't find my joke funny.

Chapter 6

Luke

When our plane landed in the nation's capitol, we got a ride to the hotel where I planned on catching up on some sleep before the meeting in the morning. After a shower, I grabbed my phone to check messages. I hadn't turned it on since we boarded the flight. When I went through the missed calls, texts, and messages, I knew sleep would have to wait. Tahiti had left five messages. She was shook up about the argument. When I seen the look on her face after she answered, I knew she needed me to ease her mind.

"Hey, baby. How are you doing?"

"I want to go home," she whined. "I don't want to be in this stupid hotel by myself. Why couldn't I come with you?"

"I already told you why. But don't worry, I'll figure everything out when I get back in town. Relax. We'll be okay."

"But I don't want to stay here all by myself, baby."

"I'm staying by myself, too. It's not that bad. Catch up on some work or TV. I'll be back in two days."

"Syncere is a bitch. I should go home and whoop her ass. She lucky I'm pregnant."

I laughed. "You crazy. Let me pause you real quick. Somebody on my other line."

"No! I don't want you to go."

"I'm just checking the call. I'll be right back," I said before switching calls. "What's up, Carla?"

"Hey, baby boy. I was wondering if you would answer. I tried calling you a few hours ago."

"I was on the plane. Had my phone off. I just got to my room."

Excitement flashed in her voice. "You in Milwaukee

already?"

"Nah. Out in DC. Got an important meeting in the morning. I'm flying your way tomorrow."

"Damn. I was hoping your ass was on your way tonight. I can't stop thinking about your dick in my ass. My pussy getting wet thinking about it."

"You ain't gotta wait much longer. I'm fucking your ass good. You be talking all this freaky shit like you can handle me. Show me when I show up. Don't be on no bullshit."

"I won't. I'ma put this pussy on your young, fine ass. Don't think 'cause I'm fifty that I don't know what I'm doing. Experience is the best teacher."

"I hear you, baby. But let me get back with you later. I gotta get some sleep. The jet lag got me tired."

"Okay, baby boy. Call me tomorrow."

After ending the call, I switched back to Tahiti.

"Damn. Took you long enough," she whined. "Who was that?"

For the briefest moment I considered lying to Tahiti, but considering what happened a few hours ago in LA, lies would only complicate things. "Do you remember Money from Waupun?"

She thought for a moment. "No. Why? Should I know him?"

"Yeah. I stabbed him at rec. Marcell Carter."

Recognition flashed in her eyes. "Oh yeah! I remember him. Why is he calling you. You stabbed him. Ham killed his guy."

"I wasn't talking to that bitch-ass nigga. That was his momma."

She frowned. "Why are you talking to his mother?"

"'Cause I'm going to Milwaukee tomorrow and fucking her. I'ma record it and send the pictures to Big Ham so he can show niggas."

She started laughing. "No, Luke! That is so wrong. Don't do it, baby."

"I already made plans. Can't go back now. I'ma show his bitch ass how I treat Calico's groupies."

***

When my flight touched down in Milwaukee, I grabbed an Uber and hit up the Four Seasons. I had just checked into my room when the phone rang. A smile crossed my face when I looked at the screen. After listening to the recording, I pressed one. "Big Ham! How you feeling, big brah?"

"You got it, brah. Still in the belly of the beast. Waiting to get this court shit over with so I can head to the feds. How you?"

"Good, my dude. Blessed. I know I told you this a million times, but I'ma tell you again. Thank you for coming through for me the way you did. Taking the weight was some real nigga shit."

He laughed. "C'mon, Luke. We ain't finna do this every time I call. We good, my nigga. I used some of that shit to start my granddaughter a college fund. You blessed me, my dude."

"That's good to hear. I won't bring it up for a couple months. But guess what? You won't believe this shit."

"What? You done bought some stock in a prison or something?"

"Nah. I'm in the hotel right now, waiting for Money's momma to come over. I popped a Viagra and I'm about to fuck her in the ass 'til she shitting everywhere."

He laughed. "Yeah right, nigga. Stop bullshitting. You about to fuck his moms, for real? On what?"

"On everything I love. And I'm recording it. I'ma send you the pictures. Make sure you pass them around and let everybody know his OG is a thot."

He laughed again. "Damn, Luke! Yo' ass ain't shit, nigga. But I'ma get them in general pop. His bitch-ass gon' be sick. Is she bad?"

"Hell nah. Average looking vet wit' a fatty. She think she still got it, so she like fucking young niggas."

"That nigga gon' be sick when them flicks touch. Make sure you bust a nut in that bitch face!"

After hollering at my boy for fifteen minute, I hit the shower to get fresh. I had just stepped out of the water and threw on a fresh, white robe when there was a knock on the door. When I opened it, Money's mom stood on the stoop trying to look sexy. She had one hand on her hip, the other holding the door frame, smiling up at me like I was the best thing smoking. In person she wasn't bad looking – average height, dark skin, hair cut in a choppy do. She wore a black cat suit that showed off her curvy figure.

"Hey, baby boy! Damn, you fine!" she grinned, leaning in for a kiss.

I turned my face, allowing her to kiss me on the cheek as I wrapped her in my arms. "Hey, Carla. Good to finally meet you. And you rocking that cat suit."

She did a twirl, making sure to poke her ass out. "Can I come in? You got something to drink?"

"Nah. I didn't have time to stop at the store. I did all of this on short notice. My girl probably looking for me right now. I don't got that much time," I lied.

Lust flashed in her eyes. "Well, what the fuck we waiting for?" she asked before pushing me on the bed.

I laid back and watched her do a sexy undress. She didn't wear a bra or panties underneath the clothes. Her breasts were saggy, and she had a few stretch marks around her midsection, but over all, her body wasn't bad. I grabbed my phone and started recording. "Yeah, baby. You know what I wanna see."

"Wait, baby boy! What you doing?" She frowned.

"I'ma need something to remember you by when I get home. Ain't no telling the next time I'll be in town, and this will keep me satisfied until we see each other again."

She gave an understanding smile. "You lucky you fine, nigga. I can't tell yo' ass no," she said before spinning around and showing her ass to the camera. And it wasn't a bad ass, considering her age. Big and round with a few lumps and dimples. Took it to the next level when she started twerking and did the splits.

"Damn, Carla. Do that shit, baby!" I cheered.

"I might be fifty, but I still got it. Now open that robe up and let me see what you working with."

I held the camera in one hand and used my free hand to open the robe. My man wasn't hard yet, but she looked at me like I had a dragon hammer.

"Oh, hell yeah!" she smiled, licking her lips as she knelt on the bed. "Stay yo' fine and sexy ass right there. I got this."

I started to protest because I had planned on fucking her in the ass and kicking her out, but something about the look in her eyes made me keep quiet. The cougar started at my chest, sucking my nipples and running her hands over my abs. She eventually licked her way down to my dick, and when she took me in her mouth, I knew the tables had turned. She worked her lips up and down my pole like an expert, using lots of spit. I held the camera in place and closed my eyes as she did her thing. She went from deep throating to sucking just the head, to deep throating me again. When she removed her mouth, I opened my eyes to see why. She moved her mouth to my balls while jacking me off. I was in awe at her skills. She licked, sucked, and hummed on my balls until I was tingling all over. When she went back to sucking me, she spit a big loogie on my shit and slurped it up as she chewed me some more. I tried as best as I could to hold off my nut, but couldn't hang on with the cougar's mouth.

"Awe shit!" I grunted, exploding in her mouth.

Carla didn't miss a beat. I could feel her throat muscles moving as she swallowed my nut. When I was drained, she lifted her head and wiped the back of her hand across her lips. "Oh, yes! And you still hard! Stay right there, baby boy. Don't move. Where your rubbers at?"

I pointed to the table. "In the drawer."

She leapt from the bed with way more agility than I expected from a fifty-year-old lady. She grabbed the box of magnums and took one out. To show me that her skills were official, she opened the wrapper and put the condom between her lips. After crawling back on the bed, she lowered her head and put the condom on me without using her hands. All mouth. I watched on my phone as she mounted my pole and rode it. Her pussy was a little tight so she started off slow, riding me steadily, closing her eyes and letting out moans. She eventually sped up the pace and started riding me so fast and hard that my head was bouncing off the bed. She came twice during the ride but didn't slow down or miss a beat.

When I busted my second nut, she changed the rubber, staring at my dick like she wanted to cut it off and take it with her. "Damn, Luke. You got some good dick, baby boy. Where your young ass been all my life?"

She didn't give me a chance to respond before she spun around reverse cowgirl and shoved my dick in her ass. She took me all the way in and sat there for a few moments to let her anal walls adjust to me. When she was ready, she rode me the same way she did when I was in her pussy, started off slow, working to a fast pace, slamming her ass onto my pelvis every time she came down. The blue pill had my dick harder than steel, and she was taking full advantage of it. I swear it felt like she rode me for thirty or forty five minutes. I got tired of recording and sat my phone aside, trying to force myself to bust a nut. She came two more times before I busted my third.

"You got some more rubbers?" she asked, ready for more.

I wiped the sweat from my brow, happy there were only two in the pack. "Nah. I told you I only had a little bit of time."

She looked disappointed. "Damn, baby boy. I hate to let a good dick go. And it don't look like you want to go because you still hard."

I looked down at my tool. He was pointed at the ceiling like a flagpole. But I didn't want any more pussy. I was good. "I see. But I need to leave. Next time I'm in Milwaukee, we gon finish this."

"I understand. Just make sure yo' fine ass call me. And send me that video. I wanna watch that later," she said while putting her clothes back on.

"You got that. You put on a hell of a show."

She was putting her shoes on when her phone rang. "Oh, this is my son. Let me answer this real quick. Hey, Money. How you doing, baby?"

I couldn't waste an opportunity to let Money know I fucked his mother. "How old is your son?"

She mouthed 'twenty-five.'

"Where he at?"

'In jail,' she mouthed again, listening to him talk.

"In prison? Which one? I might know him."

She covered up the mouthpiece. "He's in Waupun."

My eyes lit up. "I was in Waupun. I know your son. Let me holla at that nigga real quick."

"Um, hey, my friend wants to talk to you. He said he knows you."

"Money, what's good, nigga? How you been?" I asked, happy to talk to him.

"What up? Who dis?"

"This Luke, brah. What's good?"

He paused for a moment. "I don't know you, nigga."

I knew he remembered me, and I was going to add fuel to the fire. "Yes, you do, nigga. I was there when that shit happened to you and Buck. This Luke."

He paused again. "When I get out, I'm killin' you, nigga. Now put my momma back on the phone."

I ignored his request, loving the anger I heard in his voice. "Yeah, my nigga. Me and yo' moms chillin' at the telly. We gettin' close. Now, I ain't trynna be yo' daddy or nothing, but if you ever need something, hit my line."

"*Put my momma back on the phone, bitch-ass nigga!*" he screamed.

I handed her the phone. "He want you."

She took the phone and walked out.

After she left, I took a shower and thought about Carla. She came over and wrecked my dick. I wasn't expecting her to get down like that. The icing on the cake would be hearing Money's reaction after he got wind of the pictures.

Chapter 7

Syn

Fuck Luke and Tahiti!

I told that bitch not to get pregnant or fall in love. The thought of her having Luke's baby was killing me, especially since I had just lost my daughter and couldn't have kids. And they didn't even tell me! I had to find out on my own. I felt betrayed. They were keeping secrets, and I didn't like it. I wanted to hurt both of their asses. The two people I loved the most had hurt me the worst, and I wanted them to feel my pain. Being in love was some bullshit.

I grabbed my phone from the bed to check the time. 7:57 AM. I had seventeen missed calls and texts, most of them from Derikka. Synful Desires was supposed to open in three minutes, and I was still wearing the same clothes as yesterday. A half-empty bottle of Ciroc and a bottle of Oxycontin lay next to me. I felt terrible, like not going to work. Like lying in bed, popping pills all day, and drinking. Then my phone rang. It was my assistant. I cleared my throat before answering.

"Hey, Derikka."

"I've been calling you for an hour!" she panicked. "Are you okay?"

"Yeah. I'm running late. I lost my phone. Where are you?"

"I'm in the building. What time are you coming in? Mark Katon is coming to take pictures of Sevyn at 9:00. You were supposed to meet with him before the shoot."

Shit! I forgot about Mark. He was one of the most sought-after photographers in the game. His pictures were published in all the magazines. We needed to talk about that. "I know. I didn't forget. I'm checking out a property. I'll be there in an hour. Tell Mark I'll be there before he finishes the shoot. Keep everything running smoothly until I get there."

"Okay. I got it. I'll see you in a minute."

After setting my phone down, I let out a long breath. Emotionally, I was a mess. Mentally, I was slipping. On the inside my world was crumbling down. I had been walking around in a foggy daze for months, second-guessing everything I thought was real. I was a mess, and I knew it. But no one else did. I put on my brave face every time I opened my eyes or had human interaction. And I would continue to put forth my best image. Nobody would ever see me falling apart or crawling on my knees.

I'm Syncere Evans. The boss of all boss bitches. A go-getter. An independent woman who doesn't need anybody to complete or validate me. I know who I am, and I'm responsible for my own happiness.

After running the Boss Bitch mantra through my mind, I popped two Oxycontins, chased them with Ciroc, put the evidence in my purse, and then went to take a shower. I tried as best I could to wash the stain of Luke and Tahiti's betrayal from my skin as I stood under the shower mist. It didn't work. I was still thinking about whooping both they asses while I dried off.

After wrapping the towel around my body, I walked over to the best part of my big-ass house, which was my walk-in closet. One hundred square feet of clothes, shoes, and accessories. I had vanity mirrors, bright lights, and plush chairs for me to relax amongst my labels.

I was searching through a rack of dresses when I heard a noise in the hallway. I hoped it was Luke. I hadn't seen or talked to him in two days, and I had my thoughts together, ready for round two. I left the closet as Tahiti stepped into the room.

When she seen me, she paused, fear spreading over her

face. "I didn't know you were here. I thought you were at work."

I mugged her ass. "Right. You didn't see the cars in the driveway. What the fuck do you want? Why are you in my house?"

"I. Um. I just wanted to get some of my things."

I stared at her angrily. The part of me that loved her wanted to let her come home. The part of me that hated her wanted to beat her ass and kick her out. "Don't you got enough already? You got my man's baby. Luke will take care of you. You don't need nothing else from this house."

"Syncere, please. It's not what you think it is."

"What is it, Tahiti? You not really three months pregnant? You haven't been keeping this from me?"

"Syn, it's not like that. I —"

"Well, what is it like, then? Are you pregnant or not?"

"Yes, I'm pregnant."

"Why didn't you tell me?"

"I don't know. We didn't know how."

"Stop saying that shit!" I snapped. "Y'all talking all this 'Syn, I love you' shit, but keeping secrets. You should've told me. Now, what else do you want?"

She stood in front of me looking confused. And then the tears came. "I want you, Syn. I want to come home. I don't want you to be mad no more."

"You should've thought about that before you mothafuckers lied to me. I don't want you. Get out of my house."

Instead of leaving, she walked further onto the room, stopping about a foot away from me. "Can we at least talk? Don't do this."

I remained firm. "You better get out of my house before I beat your ass!"

She surprised me by getting loud and aggressive. "If you

want to fight, let's fight, then! I don't care! I tried to talk to you, but you're acting like a real bitch. What's up?"

The way she put up her hands told me Tahiti had probably never been in a fight before. If I wanted, I could've kick her ass all over the house. But she was pregnant. And I really didn't want to fight her. I wanted her to leave so I could stay mad at her and Luke.

"I told you to get out of my house. I'm not telling you again."

She stood her ground. "I'm not leaving until we talk. The quicker we talk, the quicker I'll leave."

I walked back into the closet with the towel still wrapped around my body. "I do not have time for this shit. I have to go to work."

She followed behind me. "I'm pregnant, Syn, but that doesn't mean anything changes. I'm not trying to break up what we have. I don't want to take Luke from you. I want to be with both of you. Like it's been from the beginning. The baby makes us family. And it's not just my baby. It's yours, too. The baby will have two mommies. I love you, Syn. Talk to me. Please."

I tried to act like her words didn't affect me as I searched for a panty and bra set, but they did. I could hear the sincerity in her voice, and it was comforting to know she wasn't trying to take my spot. She wanted us both. She loved me, too.

"Tahiti, you in here?" Luke called.

Hearing him call her name and not mine made me feel some type of way, but I didn't respond. I put my panties on and acted like I didn't hear anything.

"We're in the closet!" Tahiti called.

Luke showed up at the door, looking surprised. Like he expected us to be fighting. "Y'all good?"

I didn't say anything.

"She still on some bullshit. Still acting mad," Tahiti said.

That got my attention. "Nah, y'all the ones on some bullshit. Not me. Y'all lying and hiding shit. I'm acting like this because y'all muthafuckas keeping secrets."

Luke walked in the closet and stood in front of me. "We already apologized. We fucked up, baby. Now, what are we gonna do? Is this about to break us up? After everything we've been through, you're telling me this is going to be the thing that separates us? Not being shot at, me going to prison, or us having to drop bodies, but a baby?"

I ignored his question and went to get my red Gucci dress. "I don't have time for this shit right now. I have to get to work."

Luke snatched the dress and threw it against the wall. "This ain't no fucking game, Syncere! Ain't nobody going nowhere until we figure this out. You had two days to be mad. Now, what do you want to do? You saying it's over? We walking away?"

I stared up into Luke's angry eyes, having a brief reverie about the man he used to be versus the man he was today. They were night and day. I loved him more than anything or anyone I had ever loved. And he loved me, too. He proved it by killing and going to prison for me. He was my nigga. My man. My husband. My protector. My ride-or-die. My everything. And there was no way I was letting one of the best things that has ever happened to me get away.

"I'm hurt, Luke. I feel betrayed."

His face softened. "And we're sorry for that. For real. We never meant to hurt you. We love you. I love you."

"But I can't have kids, and I feel some type of way that she is having your baby. You share something with her that me and you won't ever be able to share."

He waved Tahiti over, grabbing us both by the hand. "No, baby. You have it all wrong. This is not me and Tahiti's baby. This is all of our baby. He or she will have two mothers. I will make sure your name is on the birth certificate, too. This is your baby as much as it is mine. We are family."

"I love you, Syn," Tahiti added. "I'm your girl. I'm not trying to replace you. I can't. I want to be with you and Luke. I want the baby to bring us closer and make us a real family."

Hearing their words was as comforting as wrapping a warm blanket around someone experiencing hypothermia. Their sentiments were healing and soothing. In that moment, I felt loved. But I wasn't letting their asses off the hook that easily.

"I swear to God y'all better not ever keep nothing from me ever again. If I ever feel like this again, I'm fucking y'all up! I'm handing out more than slaps next time."

"There won't be a next time," Tahiti said.

"She's right, baby," Luke added. "There won't be a next time. Now, can we kiss and make up?"

I was about to say no, but Tahiti, being the overachiever, started kissing me. Her lips were soft, tongue demanding. Then Luke grabbed my face away from her and started kissing me while Tahiti kissed and licked my neck. Having my lovers attack my body got me hot and horny, but I had an important meeting to keep.

"Wait. I have to get to work," I protested.

"You're already late," Tahiti said.

"And you can be as late as you want to be. You're the boss," Luke said, picking me up and kissing me as he took me to the bedroom.

After laying me on the bed, he attacked my body again. He removed the towel from around me, snatched my panties off and threw them across the room while Tahiti raced to get undressed. When Luke's tongue hit my clit, all thoughts of work disappeared. He was sucking, licking, and humming. I was moaning and trying to pull his face further into my pussy.

"Let me get her while you take your clothes off," Tahiti

said.

When Luke got up to get undressed, Tahiti's tongue replaced his. And my goodness, this woman knew how to eat pussy. She had me grabbing fistfuls of her hair and the bed sheets.

When Luke was naked, he moved us to the sixty-nine position with me on top of Tahiti. Then he got behind me and fucked me from behind while Tahiti sucked my clit. It felt as good as the first time I popped an Oxycontin. When I came, it was amazing. It felt like all my anger from the past two days had been crushed up and seeped out in my orgasm.

For the encore, Tahiti strapped on *Luke*, my custom strap-on dildo. They lay me on my side, Tahiti in the front, Luke behind me. If being fucked while getting my clit licked felt amazing, being fucked in both my holes upped the ante. And they didn't just have sex with me – they made love to me. Tahiti fucked me from the front, kissing me while whispering how much she loved me. Luke was kissing my neck, pulling my hair, calling me his wife and saying how much he loved fucking me in my ass. I was delirious with pleasure, and all I could do was hang on and enjoy being double-penetrated.

When I came, the second orgasm was better than the first.

Chapter 8

Luke

"I swear, your mother better not throw no shade at me today."

I looked toward the passenger seat of the rented Cadillac truck. Syn's arms were folded over her chest, a sour look on her face. "You good, baby. We're all going to have a good time this weekend. It's the Fourth of July, all about celebrating America's independence."

"We better. 'Cause I ain't taking no shit from your parents. Not this time."

"They ain't that bad, are they?" asked Tahiti.

Syn spun toward the back seat. "Yeah, to you they might not be that bad. You ain't the one getting blamed for Luke going to jail and getting shot. I'm tired of they old asses and they bullshit."

I leaned over to kiss my boss bitch on the cheek. "My wounds have healed, and I'm a free man. They know I love you, baby. We're leaving the past in the past. This year is all about being healthy and in love. No more drama."

She smirked. "Whatever, Mary J. Blige."

Nostalgia greeted me at the door when I walked into the house I had grown up in. The sight and smell of home brought memories rushing like a flashback. For a moment I thought Big Chief would come swaggering down the hallway and challenge me to a game of one-on-one basketball in the driveway.

"Daddy!" Latia screamed, running at me like a one hundred-meter sprinter about to cross the finish. She wore a pair of blue jean overall shorts that were covered in dirt.

Even though she was only ten years old, I could see the woman she would become emerging under her youthful features. Her twisties bounced, the smile on her face making

67

me wish I had recorded the moment on my phone. My baby was beautiful and smart, a straight-A student who was always on the honor role, and a cheerleader and gymnast with big plans to be in the Olympics when she turned fifteen.

"Hey, baby! Every time I see you, you get prettier," I told her, wrapping her in my arms.

"You have to come up with another compliment, Daddy. You have to be innovative. Granny says a man with culture will be good with his words."

I looked at Latia like she was speaking Swahili. "What you just say?"

"Me and Granny was talking about the shortage of good black men. She told me to look for a man that is cultured."

Syn and Tahiti laughed. I didn't find anything funny. "Where is Granny?"

"In the backyard. We planting tomatoes. Hi, Syncere! Hi, Tahiti!"

I sat my daughter down and let her kick it with the ladies while I went to find my mother. She was kneeling in a large patch of the backyard that had been dug and cultivated, working with a small shovel. Her normally light-brown complexion had been darkened by the long hours in the sun tending the garden. She wore a black shirt, shorts, and no shoes.

"Why you telling Latia to find a man with culture?"

Momma looked up from the patch of dirt she was tending, elation spreading across her features. At fifty-four years old, Momma was in good shape and had a youthful constitution thanks to the students at her high school. She also didn't take lip from nobody, so when she recognized the attitude in my voice and on my face, the elation was replaced by a motherly scold.

"Don't come up in my house fussing at me! You know I don't play that."

I turned down my attitude several notches as I walked over to the garden. She stood, eyeing me, waiting for the apology that she knew was coming.

"Sorry about that, Mom. How are you're doing?" I relented, wrapping her in a hug.

"That's much better," she smiled, hugging me back. "I'm doing fine. Me and my granddaughter planting some tomatoes. Where is your little demon floozy?"

"C'mon, Momma. We're not about to spend the weekend doing this, are we? Syncere is my girl. We are holding each other down through thick and thin. Don't make this a bad experience. It's all about love and happiness this holiday."

"Whatever, Al Green. I don't like her, and I won't ever like her. She got you shot and put in jail. I know I taught you better than to be messing with this crazy woman."

"You also taught me to follow my heart. To respect and honor my woman. And love the person that loves you. Syncere is a good woman, momma. And she's my woman. She just had a lot of baggage, but its all behind us now."

Mom rolled her eyes. "Whatever. Speaking of Satan's minion."

I looked toward the back door as Syncere, Tahiti, and Latia stepped into the backyard.

"And why are you talking to Latia about cultured men and boyfriends? She's too young for that."

Mom waved away my words. "Boy, please. In a few years she will be a young lady. I don't want her gravitating to the kinds of men her mother deals with, so I'm teaching her the difference between a cultured man and a Bone Thugs-N-Harmony."

Even though I didn't like Mom having conversations about boys with my daughter, I couldn't dispute the logic behind it. She dealt with streets niggas. One of them tried to kill me and was resting in hell. Mom was being proactive. I had to respect her position.

When my girls walked over, Mom and Syn had an uncomfortable stare down. "Hi, Mrs. Swanson," Syn managed, forcing a smile.

Mom rolled her eyes. "Girl, please."

Syn copped an attitude. "See, this is why I didn't want to come over here. You always acting like you got a problem with me."

"C'mon, y'all. Chill. We ain't on this," I tried.

"I do got a problem with you," Momma said, getting on Syncere's level. "You got my son shot and put in jail. I don't like you. And I don't want him to be with you."

"C'mon, y'all. Not right now," I tried again.

"Well, he is with me. And we're getting married. I'm not going nowhere, and neither is he. It don't matter if you don't like me because he loves me. Worry about your own man and let me worry about mine."

"*Enough!*" I yelled, getting all of their attention. "We not about to spend the weekend arguing and fighting. Syn is my girl, Mom. I love her, and that's that. Y'all don't gotta like each other, but show some respect."

The women rolled their eyes at each other before my mother turned to me. "Don't you raise your voice at me again. I don't care if you are grown. Watch your tone."

"What is all this racket about out here?"

I spun toward the house and seen my father standing in the doorway wearing a frown. Tall and bronze-skinned with a husky build, Martin Swanson was sixty-seven years old, but nothing about him was fragile or weak. Anything that needed fixing in the house, Pop fixed it. He didn't believe in wasting money on handymen. He was a military man who believed in working hard until he died.

"Your son is out here screaming at me like he lost his damn mind," Mom snitched.

Pop lumbered over, giving me a serious stare. "You raising your voice at my woman, boy?"

"C'mon, Pop. Relax. Her and Syncere acting crazy, and I'm trying to put an end to the madness before it starts."

It was like everything I said went in one of Pop's ears and right out the other. "Did you raise your voice at your momma? Don't be yelling at my wife, boy. You ain't too old for a tune-up."

Me and Pop had a stare down. In the silence of those few moments, he lectured me again, making sure I understood everything he said and everything he didn't say. When he felt he made his point, he extended a hand and smiled. "Welcome home, son. And congratulations on that accounting firm thing. Me and your mother are proud of you."

As I shook hands with my dad, I marveled at how he had gone from disciplining to congratulating me in a matter of seconds. "Thanks, Pop. Couldn't have done it without my girls. They've been my backbones," I said, nodding at Syn and Tahiti.

"Your girls?" Mom frowned.

"Hey, Mr. Swanson," Syncere waved.

"Hi, Mr. and Mrs. Swanson," Tahiti smiled.

"Hey, Syncere," Pop nodded, eyeing Tahiti before turning to me. "Who is she?"

"I was hoping that we would be able to talk about this under different circumstances, Pop, but this is Tahiti. She is our girlfriend."

My mother, father, and daughter looked like I had just told them Jesus was in the living room.

"Say what now?" Pop asked.

"How do you have two girlfriends, Luke? We didn't raise you that way," Mom said.

"It's called a polyamorous relationship," Latia said.

We all paused to stare at my ten-year-old daughter. I was

surprised at how knowledgeable she was. "What do you know about polyamorous relationships?"

She shrank back a little, uncomfortable under our stares. "I seen it on the internet, and we talked about it in school. It's more than two people in a relationship."

"I don't care what it's called. It ain't normal," Mom said.

"All this new stuff and new words is why the world is crazy," Pop added.

"And it's nasty!" Momma said, giving us the stank eye.

"It's not what y'all think it is," I defended. "We're not freaks. We are a family. And Tahiti is four months pregnant with y'all second grandchild."

Mom threw her shovel down and walked toward the house. "This is too much for me."

"Come have a beer with your old man," Pop said. "We have a few things we need to be talkin' about."

After grabbing bottles of Budweiser, Pop and I settled in the basement, a.k.a. his man cave, leaving the ladies outside to themselves. The first thing I noticed was the TV upgrade. Last time I had been down there, he had a floor-model TV from the eighties. Today he had a fifty-inch flat screen on the wall.

"'Bout time you came to your senses and got with the times. That old Sanford and Son TV was past its time."

"Get off my TV, boy. I told you, that's a heirloom. Me and your mother was talking about getting it appraised on that show, *Antique Roadshow*. She thinks it might be worth some money."

That made me pause. "Never thought about it like that, Pop. You might be onto something."

"That's what's wrong with you young people today. Think because something is old it don't got value. Let this be a lesson, son. Everything old ain't worthless."

I nodded at the truth in his words before taking a sip from

my brew.

"Now that we're over my TV, tell me about these living arrangements. You have two women, and one of them is pregnant?"

"Yeah, Pop. That's pretty much it."

"How does that work, son? Y'all all sleep together?"

I gave Pop a look. "Kinda intimate question, ain't it?"

He smiled. "I've heard of polyamorous relationships. Just never thought I'd have one in my house. When I was stationed in Korea, I knew a guy who lived with two women. Man, I thought he had it made. Until they started getting jealous. Takes a lot of maturity to maintain a relationship involving three people. You sure about this?"

"Never been surer, Pop. I love them both, they love me, and they love each other. This is real. We've been through battles. Our relationship is fireproof. We are a family."

The smile that spread across his face told I had his approval. "I think you're living every man's fantasy. If I could've had two women under the same roof when I was in my twenties, I would've done it. I hope it works out for you. And I hope I get a grandson this time. It might take your mother some time to get used to this. You know what the Bible says about homosexuality, and this is a Christian house."

***

I had been on both sides of prison visiting rooms. Just three months ago I was locked in a maximum security prison getting visits. Now I was back to being a visitor. The Terre Haute Maximum Security Prison's visiting room reminded me of Waupun's – bright lights, shiny floors, cameras in the ceiling, the serious looks on all the faces of the guards. The sights and sounds brought back memories that had changed me in ways I couldn't put into words. Being locked in a cage and treated like an animal was hard to express, but everyone who had been locked in a box understood what I felt.

"Luke! What up, boi?"

Seeing the smile on my brother's face and the elation in his eyes pushed away my thoughts on personality changes due to prison. "Big Chief!" I smiled, standing to hug my brother.

Barron felt solid under the khaki suit. Even though he was six feet tall and 235 pounds, Barron had an unassuming look. He didn't talk loud, put people down, or wear a mean mug. He was well-spoken, had good posture, and knew how to talk his way out of anything. Except prison. Ten years ago he'd been sentenced to life in the feds. Despite the extended death sentence, he kept his head up and remained strong.

"How you doing, li'l brah? It's good to see you again. It's been way too long."

"Almost three years. Now that I got all that bullshit behind me, I'm living life to the fullest. Got a baby on the way. Hopefully a boy. Life is good, Chief. I can't complain."

"I'm happy to hear that, man. And I'm happy Syn didn't shoot your ass for getting Tahiti pregnant. Props for having two wifeys. That's boss shit."

I nodded. "Learned from the best."

"And now you doing big things. I'm proud of you, li'l bro. For real. Looking at where you at today makes me happy to know all the work it took keeping you out of the streets paid off. Got your own accounting firm. I knew you would be successful."

"So, basically you saying I should thank you for whooping my ass?" I laughed.

"Absolutely. Spare the rod, spoil the child."

After sharing a laugh, he turned serious. "I didn't want to say nothing on the phone, but niggas around here been talking about Calico. He got a brother named Reign. He out of New York. Supposed to be a mob-type nigga. Definitely a plugged thug. I don't know the nigga. Shit, I didn't even know Calico had a brother. I'm trying to find out what he knows about Calico coming up missing. But a nigga like that is gon' look for answers to how his brother came up missing. I know I would."

The news was a little unnerving. I thought we were in the clear, and now my happily-ever-after bubble had been burst. "Damn. Are you serious? When is this shit gon' be over?"

"This what happens in the streets. What I was trying to keep you away from. They never found Calico's body, right?"

I had cremated his body in a burn pit and scattered the ashes in a creek. No way his remains would be found. "Nah. He's gone."

"Well, ain't nothing you can do but watch and wait."

I let out a long breath. "Yeah. I'ma look into getting us some security if things start to heat up."

"Do that. And one more thing," he said, a wide smile spreading across his face. "My lawyers are working on getting my sentence reduced. This prison reform shit that Kim K. and the others are rooting for is putting pressure on Congress. Even the president is on board. I think they about to make something happen for me."

J-Blunt

Chapter 9

Syn

I should've gone with Luke to visit Barron. I hated being in his parents house without him. Knowing they didn't like me only added to my ill will. I wanted to be celebrated, not tolerated. But Tahiti, on the other hand, was getting a warm welcome. They had warmed up to her, and she was currently in the living room having a quasi-family gathering with Luke's parents and Latia.

I was in Luke's old bedroom, pretending like I was watching TV, binge watching the R. Kelly documentary. Truth was, I didn't give a damn about the crooning pedophile. I knew that nigga had a problem when he married the R&B singer Aaliyah back in the day. The only reason I was in the room was because I didn't want to be around Luke's people. I hated them as much as they hated me. So, I sat alone, getting high on pills and drinking Ciroc.

Tahiti came into the room some time later and crawled into bed. "Why you sitting in here by yourself?"

"I'm watching the R. Kelly documentary."

"And getting drunk. Are you okay?"

"Yeah, I'm good. I can drink when I want. I'm not the one pregnant," I laughed, taking a drink from the bottle.

She pushed me playfully. "I hate you."

"If by hate you mean love, then I hate you, too."

"I was talking to Luke's mom and daddy about baby names. They want a junior if it's a boy."

I felt a tinge of jealousy at how accepting Luke's parents were of Tahiti after knowing her for only one day, but I kept it to myself. "Luke wants the same thing. I like it."

"But what if it's a girl?"

The question felt loaded, like she was leading up to

something. "What do you think the name should be?"

"What about Trinity?"

It felt like she had taken a spear and poked me in the heart. "I don't like it."

"Why not? It can be a new beginning for everybody. Now you get the opportunity to raise your daughter. This can be –"

"No, Tahiti!" I snapped, tears burning the corners of my eyes as they slid down my face. "I don't want a do-over. I don't want to replace my daughter. She's gone. That's it."

"But it doesn't have to be that way. Talk to me, Syn. I don't think you've really grieved her. We never had a funeral, and talking about it will help."

I didn't know what Luke did with Trinity's body, and I didn't want to know. I hadn't filed any missing person reports or talked to anyone about her disappearance. As far as I was concerned, she was gone. But the hole in my soul would always be there. And I wanted it to stay.

"I don't want to talk about my daughter. What don't you understand about that?"

"I don't understand why."

"Because she's gone. Talking about it won't help."

"And neither will the pills and drinking."

That got my attention. "What pills? What are you talking about?"

She called me a liar with her eyes. "The Oxycontin in your purse. I've seen them. I know you're hurting and getting drunk and high to cope. Luke doesn't know, but I do."

I wasn't sure how to respond. I thought I hid my coping habits well. "Why were you going through my shit?"

"I wasn't snooping. I was looking for your car keys when I found them. I won't say anything to Luke. This can stay between us. I want to help you heal, baby. And maybe the baby can do it. That's why I think we should name her Trinity."

78

"I don't want to talk about this," I mumbled, getting up front the bed. I needed some air. And then my phone rang. I grabbed it from the bed and checked the screen. It was a private number. I normally didn't answer anonymous calls, but I wasn't thinking straight, and I needed a distraction from thoughts of Trinity.

"Hello?"

"Syncere? Is this you?"

The voice sounded familiar, but I couldn't place it. "Yeah. Who is this?"

"Vega."

The desire for vengeance burned in my chest when her face, name, and betrayal added up. "You got some nerve calling my phone, bitch!"

"C'mon, Syn. You know you my girl. I knew you would figure a way out of that jam. Me, on the other hand, I'm not as smart or gangsta-fied as you are. Staring down the barrel of a gun is scary as fuck. But I see you're still alive. Can't say the same for Calico. Ain't nobody heard from him."

"Loyalty is worth dying for, bitch. I saved your fucking life. Rain was about to kill your ass. And this is the thanks I get? You told Calico about me and my daughter."

"He was going to find out anyway. I wasn't going to die because she got caught. I'm smarter than that. But that ain't the reason I called. I got some good information you need to know."

My emotional state combined with the drugs and alcohol didn't allow me to think clearly about what she was saying. "Fuck you and whatever information you have. When I see you, you better duck, you ugly-ass bitch!"

"Wait, Syn! Don't hang up. You need to hear this. This could be life or death. I know I was wrong for telling Calico about Trinity. And now I'm calling to make it up to you. Just hear me out."

"What you gotta say, bitch? It better be good."

"Calico got a brother."

A cold chill ran through my body, but I acted like I was unaffected by the news. "Yeah, and?"

"He's been asking questions. And if you think Calico was a beast, his brother is ten times worse."

I wanted to hang up the phone, go find her, and blow her brains out, but I wanted to know more about Calico's brother first. "Who is he? Where he at?"

She laughed. "Now, Syn, I know you're smarter than to think I'ma just give you that information. How do I know you won't still get at me after I tell you what I know?"

"You don't. But you're already on my shit list, and I don't think you want to make it worse."

"I agree. Which is why I called. I have a proposition. Forget about my betrayal and give me twenty thousand dollars. I'll help you get him."

It was my turn to laugh. "Bitch, are you smoking dope? You think I'm going to pay you after you fucked me over? You owe me."

"Syn, listen to me. His brother is really plugged in. Calico was a small-timer compared to him. In a war, information about the enemy is more valuable than anything. Besides, it's not like you don't have the money."

Her misquote of one of the principles in the Art of War made me check my anger. I didn't want to pay the price, but I needed to know what she knew. So I played her game. "As much as I hate your ass right now, I have to admit you have a point. I'll play your game. You'll get the money. Tell me who he is."

"It's not that easy, baby. I need the cash in my hand. Face-to-face."

"I'm not at home right now. I'm out of town for the fourth. Give me your number and I'll call you when I get back home."

"I'll do you one better. I told you I'm the better chess player. I'm three moves ahead. I'll call you in three days with the meet time and location. Don't be on no bullshit."

After hanging up the phone, I let out a long breath. Just when I thought I could sit back with my family and enjoy life, fate had twisted everything. Calico had a brother who was worse than him, and Vega had a powerful set of keys that could determine the outcome.

"You okay?" Tahiti asked.

"No. I'ma step outside. I need some air."

"Wait, Syn. Don't shut me out. I'm a part of this family. I know –"

"I said I got it!" I snapped before leaving the room.

I walked through Luke's parent's house in a daze. I needed my man by my side to help me figure this shit out, but he was visiting his brother in Indiana. I planned to call him once I made it outside.

I had almost made it to the back door without incident when I ran into Mrs. Swanson in the kitchen. I hoped she wouldn't acknowledge my presence, but that would've been too kind.

"I thought you were going to stay in that room all night. You too good to hang out with the common folk?" she asked, her voice dripping with sarcasm.

I stopped at the back door to give her a dose of her own medicine. "Can't get nowhere hanging with the commoners. All they do is tear each other down with their crab-in-the-bucket mentality. I'm a eagle, Mrs. Swanson. I fly solo."

"More like a turkey buzzard," she quipped. "You're not about to get the last laugh at this. Not in my house."

"I bet you was one of those mothers that thought no girl was ever good enough for your sons. Hate that he made a good decision on his wife without your input or approval, don't you?"

"You're not his wife, nor are you good enough for my son. I hate seeing my kids make bad decisions. I thought he learned his lesson from Shay. Obviously not."

"I'm a millionaire, Mrs. Swanson. Don't compare me to some hood rat. I could buy your life. My house is worth five of yours. I did seventeen years in prison and came out and did better than you. You are a miserable old lady living a miserable old life. You need a makeover and a new wardrobe. In here looking like Madea."

Her eyes got really small, nostrils flaring. "Listen here, you project ho! Ain't no amount of money going to stop you from being an ugly person. And I hope Luke wakes up and leaves your ass for Tahiti. She's younger and prettier, and she's having his baby. When are you going to give me a grand baby? Oh, I'm sorry. You can't."

"Bitch!" I barked and made a move toward her. I didn't care if she was Luke's mother, I was going to beat her ass!

Mrs. Swanson was ready for me. She turned and grabbed a big ass knife from the block. "C'mon, bitch! Take another step toward me and I'ma cut your ass in half!"

We had a stare down, her eyes reflecting pure hatred. I returned the look times ten, wishing I had a pistol.

"Granny, can you –" Latia said, entering the kitchen and pausing when she seen our hostile looks and her grandmother holding the knife. "Are y'all okay?"

"Yes, baby," Mrs. Swanson said, putting away the knife. "I was just showing her the cutlery set you granddaddy bought me last year."

I left without another word. When I got to the rental truck, I texted Tahiti and Luke, letting them know I was spending the night at a hotel.

Chapter 10

Luke

After paying and tipping the Uber driver, I grabbed my luggage and walked through the glass double doors of the Pfister Hotel. I was greeted warmly at the desk by a young receptionist. Her name tag read Morgan.

"Hey, Morgan. I'm Luke Swanson. I need the key for room 107." I handed her my driver's license.

"One moment, Mr. Swanson," she said, turning to check the computer. After verifying my identity, she retrieved a key from the desk drawer. "Yes. Your wife said to give you the key. Here you are."

After an elevator ride to the top floor, I made my way to the penthouse suite. As soon as I opened the door, I was greeted by the magnificent smells of Tahiti's cooking. I found her in the kitchen, getting down on the stove. Cheese eggs, grits, French toast and sausage patties. And she set it all off with a French maid outfit, fish net stockings, and black heels. No panties or bra. She hadn't noticed me yet, so I paused to watch her. She looked beautiful. The pregnancy had her skin glowing and hair shining. And her body was getting thicker in all the right places. When she bent over to stir the grits, my dick jumped, hungry for his own meal.

I was so caught up in watching Tahiti that I didn't see or hear Syn coming from he bathroom. "What do you want to eat first? Her or breakfast?"

I spun toward my girl and seen her rocking a terrycloth robe and smelling like soap. "Do I get a third option?" I asked, wrapping her in my arms and getting some tongue.

"Yes, you do. So save room for dessert."

"Hey, Lukey baby!" Tahiti said, bouncing over to give me a kiss. "Do you like?" she asked, spinning and striking a few poses to show off the French maid costume.

I spoke the only French word I knew. "*Oui.*"

After sharing a laugh, I sat at the table to have breakfast with my women. "How is Barron?" Syncere asked.

"He good. Got his lawyers working to get him out. I hope it all works out. I would love to have that nigga back home."

"Kim K and Trump finally did something right," Syn quipped.

"When am I going to get to meet him?" Tahiti asked.

"I told him to add you to his visitors' list. We should have the form by the time we get back home. Now, tell me why y'all in this hotel again."

Syncere shook her head from side to side. "Yo' momma crazy."

"She pulled a knife on her," Tahiti added.

"Yeah, right," I laughed between bites of my eggs. "My mother didn't pull a knife on nobody. Quit lying."

"I don't know who you think your mother is, but whatever image you got in your head, you need to change it. Ask Latia. She seen her with the knife."

I laughed again. "I'll talk to her later. Damn. I gotta find a way to get y'all past this."

"And I need you to finish eating breakfast so we can have dessert," Tahiti said, stuffing a sausage into my mouth. "I swear, I been so horny ever since you got me pregnant."

"I can't satisfy her, baby," Syn admitted. "I tried last night. Now it's your turn."

As far as I was concerned, breakfast was over. I had my fill of food, and now I was hungry for some pussy. I pushed my chair back, pulling Tahiti on my lap, and pawing at her body as we made out. Syn moved dishes out of the way, clearing most of the table. I laid Tahiti on her back, spread her legs, and pulled my chair closer to the table. Her pussy was beautiful – Brazilian waxed, already wet, and it smelled like flowers. I grabbed the bottle of honey, poured some over her pussy, and licked it off. She made beautiful noises as I lapped at her pussy. Shit was music to my ears. I loved the way her juices tasted mixed with honey.

When Syncere got tired of watching, she pulled Tahiti's titties out, poured honey on them, and began sucking. Since she was kneeling on the table with her ass a few inches away from me, I reached my hand up and began fingering her pussy. Syn was hot as an oven and super wet. My dick was super hard and I wanted to bust a nut, but I had to finish what I started with Tahiti.

As if she was reading my mind, Syn got up from sucking Tahiti's breasts, grabbed the bottle of honey, and crawled under the table. She unbuckled my pants, pulled out my dick, poured on some honey, and swallowed me. Being in her mouth felt good as fuck. Hearing Tahiti moan my name was the icing on the cake. My nut came faster than I wanted, and I exploded in Syn's mouth. She didn't waste anything, kept sucking until I got my second wind. And that's when Tahiti reached her peak. She pulled my face deeper into her pussy until her orgasm passed.

When Syn's lips let go of my dick, she left the kitchen. I stood to undress. Tahiti watched me from the table, looking at my dick like it was the present from Santa Claus she always wanted. I threw one of her legs on my shoulder and spread the other one wide as I penetrated my baby momma. The saying about pregnant pussy being the best pussy rang in my mind as I dug her out.

Syn came back a few moments later with a vibrator and climbed on the table, sitting her pussy on Tahiti's face like they were going to sixty-nine while teasing Tahiti's clit with the vibrator as I fucked her. My BM went wild, grunted, moaned, and screamed like a woman possessed. When she came, I flipped her over and hit it from the back while Syn lay on the table and Tahiti ate her pussy and used the vibrator.

I don't know how long we fucked on that kitchen table, but when we all got ours, we retreated to the shower to clean up. Syn and I were in the room getting dressed when I remembered something me and Big Chief spoke about.

"Me and Chief talked about Calico. Turns out he has a big brother."

Syn didn't look surprised. "I know. Vega called me last night and told me. She says she knows who he is and how to find him."

That got me hot. "Vega bitch-ass called you? Seriously?"

"Yeah. Bitch want me to pay her twenty thousand for the info. She wants to meet when we get back to LA."

"If I see that bitch, I'm killing her. What did she say?"

"Nothing. She wouldn't even say his name. Wants to tell me in person. Just says he's a beast and Calico wasn't shit compared to him."

"His name is Reign, and he from New York. I looked him up. Nigga is rich. And he does some charity work. Owns a club. I didn't see shit about him being a gangster."

"Well, if he's Calico's brother…"

Syn paused when Tahiti walked in the room. Our abrupt silence made her suspicious. "What?"

"Nothing, baby. I heard you talked with my parents about baby names. What y'all come up with?" I asked, switching subjects.

Tahiti gave me a suspicious look. "Nah. Don't do that. What was you and Syncere talking about before I walked in? Did something happen?"

"No," Syn cut in. "Me and Luke was just talking."

"About what?"

"About something that has nothing to do with you."

Tahiti got mad. "Why do you always do this? I thought we were family? Why do you keep things from me? I heard y'all talking about Calico. What about him? I thought he was dead."

I tried to dead the issue. "He's gone, baby. We good. End of story."

Tahiti wasn't having it. "Stop doing that shit! I'm not a little kid. I'm in this with you, too. Stop keeping shit from me. I know Syn killed Calico and Trinity. I'm not stupid. Are we in danger? Tell me."

"Check yourself, baby." Syn eyed Tahiti. "Know your place. If we don't tell you something, it's for your own good. Leave it alone. It's over."

"So my place is to fuck, work, cook, and have babies, but I can't be in the loop on certain shit? I thought I was family? What, y'all don't trust me?"

"It's not that, baby. Me and Syncere have been through a lot, and we don't think you should know everything. For safety reasons. The less you know, the better."

Tahiti crossed her arms over her chest and stared at us. "Am I in this family or not? Do y'all love me or not?"

"You know we love you, girl. And we are family."

"Then don't leave me out. I'm in this 'til the end. Ride or die. I proved that by fucking your ass while you were in prison."

I looked at Syncere. "She has a point, baby. Calico has a brother. Vega trynna extort us for the information. We're discussing our next move."

"Damn. Is this shit going to ever be over?" Tahiti complained.

"It don't seem like it," Syn breathed. "And this nigga supposed to be worse than Calico."

Tahiti looked worried. "This doesn't sound good. What are we going to do?"

"Nothing we can do now," I jumped in. "Syn, you might have to take her up on that meeting when we get back home.

Find out what she knows. We can get that bitch missing later. If she got something that could give us the advantage, we gotta get on that."

"I was thinking the same thing. See what her ugly ass know, and then fuck her over later.

***

The Fourth of July festivities with the family were held in Washington Park. Family members I hadn't seen since before I went to prison showed up, and a good time was had by everyone except Syncere. She spent most of the evening off by herself, only kicking it with Tahiti and Latia. After a few games of basketball, I found her sitting alone, getting shade from a big oak tree.

"You look like you're having a miserable time," I laughed, sitting in the grass next to her.

"I'm fine," she slurred. "As long as you and Tahiti are good, I'm good."

"How much have you had to drink?"

"Just two wine coolers. Why?"

I stared at her for a moment. She was wasted, slurring her words, eyes glazed. "You sure? Seems like you lit."

"Yes. I'm good. Why you so worried about me?"

"Because it's still early. Don't get drunk and pass out."

"I'm good, baby. I promise. I won't drink no more. Now, go finish having fun. I'm good."

After enjoying spending time with the family, me and my girls jumped back in the Cadillac truck, headed for the hotel. I was behind the wheel, stopped at a red light when a blue Nissan blew through the intersection doing about sixty miles an hour. Four people were in the car. When I seen the driver, I couldn't believe my eyes.

A second later a police car followed, pursuing the

speeding car.

"Damn! They on them niggas' ass!" Tahiti said, excitement in her eyes as she sat up in the seat.

"I think I know the driver," I mumbled, turning to follow the chase.

"What are you doing?" Syn asked.

"I think that was my nigga, J-Murder. I'm following to see if it is."

"Them niggas in that car going to jail. I don't want us to get caught up in that."

"We won't. I just want to see how it plays out."

I could tell Syn wanted to say more, but I planned on seeing this out. A couple blocks later the Nissan crashed and the niggas inside scattered like roaches. The police hopped out and chased the slowest runner while I followed the driver.

"Luke, what the fuck are you doing?" Syn questioned.

"That's my li'l nigga. If we get into some shit with Vega and Reign, we might need him. Trust me on this, baby."

"There he go!" Tahiti pointed.

I looked and seen a skinny, dark-skinned nigga had just come out of a yard, looking around for the police. He was of average height and dressed in black clothes with nappy hair. I pulled up a few feet from him and mashed the brakes. He pulled a pistol, ready to shoot.

"J-Murder! Chill, nigga! It's Luke."

His eyes shown surprise and disbelief. "Luke, on what that's you, nigga?"

"It is. Get in! Hurry up!"

Tahiti opened the door and he jumped in just as a police car rounded the corner.

"Speed up, nigga!" J-Murder panicked.

"We good, nigga. They didn't see you get in. What the fuck you running from the police for?"

"Fuckin' wit' some ho-niggas. We was supposed to be on

a move, but shit didn't turn out right, so I had to pop a nigga. Twelve ran up on a humbug and almost booked a nigga. When the fuck you get out? I thought you had life?"

"Shit, I did. I got off on appeal. What about you? What happened to the body you was facing?"

"I did a year up north. Ran into a real nigga that wasn't getting out. Gave him five racks to write a affidavit to say he did it. He jumped at that money. Shit rough for niggas up north, doing them long bids."

I laughed, my situation with Big Ham playing in my head. "That's crazy. I had a similar situation. Ran into a real nigga that showed me love."

"Thank God for real niggas," Syn cut in.

"These my girls, Syn and Tahiti. Y'all, this my li'l nigga, J-Murder. We was cellies in the county jail when I was fighting those charges."

"Hey, J-Murder," they waved.

He looked at Syn. "I remember you from the pictures. But you said girls. Like, girlfriends?"

"Yes, girlfriends," Tahiti spoke up. "I see you out here on that hot boy shit."

"I'm trynna get a bag, shorty. It's real out here. I'ma get mines."

"It's a better way to get it than robbing niggas," Syncere said.

"Street shit all I know. I'ma die in these streets. I'm Trigga Klan. Dying ain't shit but a permanent nap."

"How you feel about moving to LA? What you doing here?"

His voice got high pitched. "Los Angeles? California?"

"Yeah, where all the stars at. Hollywood. That's where we live. We on our way to the hotel to get our shit before getting on the plane. We came to the Mil for the Fourth," I explained.

"Man, I don't know shit about LA. What I'ma be doing? This street shit is all I know."

"I need a nigga with your skills. You know Trigga was my nigga. You Trigga Klan, and I need a shooter. A storm might be coming my way, and I need a nigga on my team that will get down with me. Money ain't no problem. Car, house, expenses is all on me."

I could hear the smile in J-Murder's tone. "Shit, I'm ready right now! Dawg, could y'all introduce me to one of the Kardashians? She just broke up with Tristan, and I need to get in that family, for real."

J-Blunt

Chapter 11

Syn

I didn't like walking into Elon by myself, but I didn't have a choice. Vega wanted me to come alone. The restaurant was popular in LA and was always packed with entertainers. A person had to get reservations to even be seated, which was why she wanted to meet here. Bitch knew she was safe with people around.

After speaking with the maître d', I was escorted to the back. Vega sat in a booth wearing a money-green suit, looking black and ugly as ever. Next to her was Sofia, my Mexican ex-lover.

"Glad you could make it," Vega smiled.

I mugged her. "Don't play with me, bitch. This ain't no happy reunion. You fucked me over. You lucky I didn't come in here shooting."

"C'mon, Syncere. Can't we let that be water under the bridge?"

"Yeah, Syn. Why don't you let it go and start over," Sofia added.

If looks could kill, Sofia would've been twelve feet in the dirt. "I wasn't talking to you. This is between me and Vega. Fall back," I said before turning to the ugly pimp. "You can't burn a bridge and expect me to send a yacht. Quit playing. Tell me what I need to know so I can get the fuck out of here."

The light in her eyes dimmed and she got serious when she seen the pleasantries were over. "Okay. You got my money?"

I pulled the bank bag from my purse. "That's ten thousand. You'll get the other ten after you tell me about Reign."

Mistrust shown in her eyes. "I never told you his name.

And ten thousand wasn't the deal. Twenty up front."

"I just told you what it is. I'll give you the rest after you tell me. You're not the only one with connections, so your information better be good."

The smile returned to her face, dollar signs in her eyes. "I forgot how smart you was. Okay. His name is Reign. He's from New York, and he's plugged. Heard he a part of a secret mafia organization. The city loves him, everybody from trappers to the mayor. And he got security. Real military-trained people. He ain't to be fucked with."

I waited for her to continue. She didn't.

"That's all? You expect me to give you twenty thousand for that? You don't have an address or phone number?"

Her serious face returned. "I just told you somebody is trying to kill you. That's worth something. Can't nobody get his address or phone number. I didn't find him, his assistant found me."

I put the money back in my purse and stood to leave. "Do it look like I got 'fool' stamped on my forehead? You better hope I don't see you again. If I do, you better duck, bitch!"

***

Bringing J-Murder to LA turned out to be a good move. When I left the restaurant, he was able to follow Vega and Sofia around the city, eventually following them to their home in the valley. He kept an eye on them for three days, turning out to be the perfect bloodhound. He learned all Vega's moves and gave me all the information I needed to make my move.

"You want me to come with you?" Luke asked.

"I got it, baby. This one is on me. I should've let Rain kill her bitch-ass while we was in prison. This is my mess, and I'm about to clean it up."

We were sitting in a rented Buick a few houses down from Vega's. It was almost midnight, and the block was deserted. I was about to go handle my business. No extravagant plots, kidnappings, or drive-bys. I was going up to her house and giving it to her on the front porch. But the look Luke was giving me made me pause.

"What, baby?"

"I love yo' ass, girl, and I respect the gangsta in you. I love that you will get down and put in work. Shit, I never knew I liked that in my woman 'til I met you."

Damn, I loved this nigga. His words had an effect on me. He always knew what to say, how to say it, and when to say it. "I love you, too, baby. And I'm not a gangsta. Get it right. I'm a Boss Bitch. Boss Bitches know how to make moves."

"Well, make your move and get your boss-ass back to the car. I still think we should've let J-Murder get his gun dirty, but I get it. It's personal. I felt the same way when I bodied Silk while I was locked up. Give me a kiss and go take care of that business."

Our lip lock was more than a peck on the lips. It was a 'be safe, I'm nervous for you, hurry up and get your ass back to the car, I love you' kiss. And then I was off to put in work.

The Glock was snug against my hip as I strolled down the block and up to Vega's door. I wore black gloves, black Nike's, black jeans, and a long-sleeved black shirt. My hair was pulled into a ponytail. My heart pounded like an 808 bass drum as I walked up on the porch. According to J-Murder, Vega was home alone. She had dropped off Sofia over an hour ago. This was the perfect opportunity to strike.

I pressed the doorbell. A musical chime played. A couple moments later there was movement behind the door.

"Who is it?" Vega called, sounding far away.

I made my voice deep. "Is Vega here?"

"Who's looking?" she asked, sounding closer but not

directly in front of the door.

"I need to holla at you. Open the door."

"You better say who the fuck you is before I let my pistol do the talking!" she threatened, sounding like she was in front of the door.

I guessed she was checking the peephole, and she wasn't going to open the door. I had to make my move, so I pulled the Glock and pointed it where I thought her chest would be.

The pistol kicked three times as I squeezed the trigger. There was a scream and then shooting from the other side of the door. Wood splinters flew as Vega unleashed a volley of bullets. After flinching and ducking, I did the only thing I could do. Run.

Luke pulled up to the curb and opened the door. "What happened?" he asked, speeding away.

"She wouldn't open the door, but I got her ass. I heard her scream."

He looked unsure. "I heard shooting coming from the house. Damn, baby. If that bitch survived...."

He didn't need to finish saying the words. I knew what he was about to say, and I felt the same way. If Vega survived, we might be headed for all kinds of trouble.

A Gangster's Syn 3

Chapter 12

Luke

"Your guy is a fool!" Syncere laughed, slurring her words.

We were in The Den of Syn, standing by the bar. My ex-cellmate was in a booth with three women. Lexi, Fettish, and Syren wore next to nothing as they danced around and on J-Murder. Syncere had told her girls to show him a good time, and he was enjoying their talents.

"I don't know if his heart can handle all that fun. Nigga might have a heart attack," I laughed. "I'ma go make sure he good."

Syn gave me a look. "Right. That's why you're going over there. To check on your boy's heart. Don't got nothing to do with Fettish's big-ass booty."

I wrapped my arms around my girl's waist and pulled her close. "Don't tell me you're getting jealous of your workers?"

"Psh! Stop playing, nigga," she sassed. "None of these bitches got shit on me. Ever since I put this pussy on your mustache, you ain't been the same."

I laughed. "You know you was whipped on my shit first. Had your ass begging me to make you cum."

She kissed my lips. "Mm. Those were some good times, weren't they? And don't act like I didn't have your ass begging, too. Had you worshipping my pussy. Queen Syncere, nigga!"

"Bet you wouldn't be talking this shit if we was at home," I challenged, ready to go home and start an all-night fuck session.

A lustful smile crossed her lips. "Don't meet me there. Beat me there."

"When are you going home?"

"Tonight is a late night. I'm closing. You have some

97

time," she said before looking at her phone. "Duty calls." She stepped away from me and tripped, almost busting her shit.

I grabbed her arm to break the fall. "You okay, baby?"

She lay against me, giggling, eyes glossed over. "Damn. You saved me, baby. I'm good. Let me go so I can take this call."

I held onto her a little longer, staring into her eyes. She was wasted again. This was becoming a common thing with her, and I wasn't feeling it. "You sure you okay? How much you had to drink?"

"Not that much, Dad," she laughed. "Just a little bit. I'm fine."

After another staring contest, I let her go. She stumbled toward the office, and I went over to check on J-Murder.

"You enjoying yourself, nigga?"

He slapped Fettish's big-ass, dark-skinned booty, smiling while watching it jiggle. "Luke, my nigga, I think I'm in love!"

I copped a seat next to him and poured a glass from the bottle of Remy Martin sitting on the table. "Be careful, nigga. Fettish don't love nothing but green bills."

The dark-skinned stripper/dancer gave me an eye. "And street niggas."

"She love me, my nigga!" J-Murder laughed.

I partied it up with my boy for a little longer before retiring to my BMW. J-Murder hopped in the passenger seat. "What happened to your newfound love? You ain't bringing her with you?"

"Bitch was talking that love shit for tips. She got a whole nigga at home. And three kids. That shit was fun while it lasted. Bitch too thotty for me. I need something with some class. Like Trista."

Trista was one of Syn's models. We introduced them on his first day in town. "Don't tell me Trigga Klan's finest got a soft heart," I joked.

"Stop playin', nigga. My heart made of stone. Don't love nothing but my pistol, my money, and my niggas. And some food. Let's stop and grab something to eat before we hit the crib."

A couple minutes later I stopped at Mason's, a popping soul food/Mexican restaurant. After placing our orders, we sat in the car to wait. I was bobbing my head to Nipsey Hussle's song *Dedication* when a black Jeep Cherokee parked next to me. A tall, light-skinned woman with a curly blonde afro climbed from behind the wheel. J-Murder looked like he had fallen in love again.

"You good, nigga?" I laughed.

He continued to ogle the woman. She had a slim build and wore a flowery top with short shorts that showed off long legs. "Nah, brah. I gotta have that," he said before climbing from the car.

I watched as he followed the woman into the restaurant, sparking a conversation. Then my phone vibrated. It was a text from Tahiti. She was home alone and horny as ever. I entertained her with a few minutes of sexting. When I looked up again, J-Murder and the woman had come back outside. She was leaning against the wall, smoking a cigarette.

Motion at the restaurant's doors got my attention. Two niggas with long dreadlocks walked out eyeing J-Murder's new friend. I could see words exchanged, but I couldn't hear what was being said. Then one of them walked toward J-Murder like he wanted an issue. The woman stepped between them, attempting to keep them apart.

I was climbing from the car when it went down. The nigga with the issue pushed the woman, making her stumble and fall. J-Murder swung twice. Both punches connected with the stranger's face, sitting him on his ass. When his friend tried to get involved, the woman kicked out a leg, tripping him.

The one that got knocked on his ass reached for his waist, but he was too slow. The blonde-haired, long-legged vixen already had her gun out, pointed at his chest. "Don't even think about it," she threatened. "Put your hands up!"

"Ay, baby, chill! Don't be like that," he said, lifting his hands in the air.

"Don't neither one of y'all move," she ordered, keeping the gun on the wannabe thugs as she stood to her feet. "I'm Officer Lewis with the LAPD. Y'all picked the wrong one to fuck with. Today is my day off, and I just wanted something to eat. Take his gun," she told J-Murder, who did as he was told. "Now, since I don't feel like taking y'all asses to jail and filling out paperwork, I'ma give y'all five seconds to get the fuck out of my face. Don't let me see y'all punk asses no more or I'm locking y'all asses up!"

Lil Wayne and 2 Chainz scrambled up from the ground, hopped in an old school Monte Carlo, and peeled out.

I was surprised she was the police and impressed by her fearlessness. J-Murder stared at her like he had fallen under a love spell.

"You don't have to look at me like that, Jason," she said, calling J-Murder by his real name.

"I don't know why, but that shit was sexy as fuck! Turned me on," he laughed. "You sure you don't want to kick it with me for the night?"

"I'm sure, man. Now give me that. I don't want you to end up in trouble with it." She held her hand out for the gun J-Murder had taken from them.

"Here you go." He handed it over. "You sure you don't wanna change your mind about kicking it with me tonight?"

"Yes, I'm sure. They just spoiled my appetite. I think I'll have them deliver the food to my house. You have a good night. Call me some time," she said before hopping in her Jeep and driving away.

"Damn. That was some shit, wasn't it? I see you got them hands," I laughed.

J-Murder continued to watch her Jeep as she drove away. "Damn, my nigga. I think I just fell in love."

***

"I don't know if I want to have a baby shower. Ain't that for family and friends to do for me?" Tahiti asked.

"Nah, baby. You plan your own shower. Plus, we don't have many family and friends in LA. All we got is us."

We were at her doctor's appointment. She was getting a check-up and ultrasound. Today we would learn if we were having a boy or girl.

Tahiti looked up from the exam table, her eyes lighting up. "I have an idea."

Her look told me this might be good. "What you got, baby?"

"I think we should do a baby shower and gender reveal party all in one. And we can do it at The Den of Syn."

I thought for a moment. "I'm cool with the baby shower at the club, but I need to know if I'm having a son today. I can't wait no more. I already been waiting five months."

"But that will make everything more exciting. C'mon, baby. Let's wait to find out. Please. I don't want to know right now."

I wasn't convinced. "Nah, baby. I can't wait any longer. I already got the jitters. I need to know today."

She slid off the table and walked over to me, pleading with her eyes. "Please, Luke. Let's wait. That way my parents – well, my mom at least – can fly out from Minnesota. You and Syn can finally meet her. It will be worth the wait. Please!"

I wasn't sold on the idea, but I also didn't want to take the joy out of the experience of childbirth for the first-time mother. "Tell you what. I'ma call Syn and let her decide. She can be the tie-breaker."

Tahiti was giddy, jumping up and down as I called Syn on the speaker phone.

"Hey, baby. What are we having?" she answered.

"We don't know yet. We waiting on the doctor," Tahiti said. "But I was thinking we should wait to find out what we're having. We could have a gender reveal party and baby shower at the same time in The Den of Syn. And we can fly out my parents so y'all can meet them."

"That's not a bad idea. What did Luke say?"

"I want to know right now," I spoke up. "But I don't want to take the fun and surprise out of it all, so we're letting you decide. No pressure."

"Awe, man. Why y'all gotta put this on me," she whined.

"I thought you would relish making the final decision, you being a Boss Bitch and all," I laughed.

"You know what, Luke? For being such a smartass and telling that corny-ass joke, I'm with Tahiti. We're waiting until the party to find out."

"Yes! Yes!" Tahiti celebrated.

I shook my head and sulked. "Just so y'all know, I'm putting y'all on dick restriction for a month. No Luke."

"What do you think we did while you was locked up?" Syn laughed.

"You the one that's gon' be missing out. This pregnant pussy is delicious," Tahiti added.

The room door opened and in walked the doctor. "Syncere, we'll call you back. The doctor is here."

"Good afternoon Ms. Johnson and Mr. Swanson," Doctor Peggy Lieberman smiled. She was an older white woman with blonde hair and green eyes. "Are we ready to find out the sex of the baby?"

"We're going to wait," Tahiti said, smiling way too hard. Peggy looked to me.

"We're going to have the gender reveal during the baby shower," I mumbled halfheartedly.

The doctor melted with sentimentality. "Oh! That is a good idea! It will be such a wonderful surprise. I've had several patients that have done gender reveal parties. They all loved it. If you step on the scale, Tahiti, I'll get your weight before checking you and the baby's vitals."

After getting her weight checked, Tahiti lay on the table and lifted her shirt. After putting jelly on her pregnant belly, the doctor grabbed the ultrasound device and rolled it across the jelly. It didn't take long to find the baby's heartbeat. "He or she has a very strong heartbeat," the doctor said.

While Peggy continued to guide the wand across her belly, I watched the monitor intently, trying to figure out the sex of the baby. It was like trying to decode Sanskrit. The screen looked like a black and white painting done by a toddler. When I realized I didn't know what the hell I was looking at, I asked for help. "Hey, Doc. Any chance you can just tell me what the baby is and keep it between us?"

She laughed, shaking her head. "Sorry, Luke, but I have to respect the wishes of the mother. Just wait it out. It'll be fun."

J-Blunt

Chapter 13

Luke

I loved fucking Tahiti. Her movements. Her Moans. Her kisses. Her wetness. It felt like her body was made for me. She fit perfectly against me, and my dick fit perfectly in her pussy. Every time I pushed forward, she threw that ass back at me, taking as much as I was giving. I had one hand on her hip, the other spreading that phat ass apart, focused on hitting that left wall.

"Oh yeah, baby! Right there! Hit it right there, nigga!" she urged.

Hitting Tahiti from the back was like watching a sunrise for the first time. Magnificent. Her ass bounced against my pelvis, jiggling like Jell-O. It got so good that I wanted to watch her work.

"Wait, baby. It's on you," I said, pulling out and lying on my back. "Let me watch that ass jiggle."

"I got you, baby. You know I'm the number one rider."

She slid onto my pole reverse cowgirl, taking me all the way in. Then she leaned forward and rode me slowly so I could watch my dick disappear in slow motion. When she got in the zone, she bounced that ass on me like a porn star, tugging and massaging my balls. Shit felt way too good.

"Damn, baby. Yo' pussy is on fire!" I moaned, trying to hold back my nut. She was making it hard.

"Wait, baby. I want to look in your eyes when you nut inside me."

That's why I loved fucking her. She knew how to get me there on every level. And after spinning around, she rode me straight up, kissing me and staring in my eyes. Watching her fuck face was erotic and sexy as fuck. When I busted my nut, my toes tingled like I was having a stroke.

"I love fucking you, nigga," she sang between kisses.

"I was just thinking the same thing. Damn, we struck it gold with you."

"One in a million, baby. Ride-or-die and a rider. You ain't neva had a bitch like me."

I thought about everything Tahiti had done for me. Truly a down-ass bitch. "I won't ever forget everything you did while I was locked up. You held me down times ten."

"You bet not ever forget. And you know what? I would do it all over again if we had to. Being with you and Syn is one of the best things that has happened to me in a long time. I never imagined I could fall in love with two people, let alone a woman. But I have. And it feels amazing. And I really love the way you fuck me, so hurry up and get back in the game. You know Syncere will come home ready to fuck. Plus, I need to get some more. Five orgasms a day help the baby come out easier."

I laughed. "You just made that shit up, didn't you?"

"I did. But it sound good, don't it."

"Crazy ass," I said as my phone rang. "Hand me that. Who is it?"

Tahiti grabbed the phone from the bedside table and lay next to me, reading the screen. "A text from the Boss Bitch. She wants you to call."

We hit her on FaceTime. "Hey, baby. We was just talking about you," I grinned.

"Look like y'all was having a party without me."

"I drained them balls, baby," Tahiti laughed. "But I saved some for you. Better hurry up and come home."

Syn gave a strained smile. Something was wrong.

"What's up, baby? You good?"

"She survived."

Even though she didn't say her name, I knew who 'she' was. "How do you know?"

"She sent me a message. Actually, left me a voicemail. Stupid bitch. She said 'it's on.'"

The worst thing that could've happened had actually happened. "Damn, baby. This is fucked up."

"Don't you need somebody to watch out for you?" Tahiti asked. "What if they on the way to get you now?"

"I thought about that. I don't know who she know in LA. The bitch do got a little money, so she might be able to pay somebody."

I let Tahiti have the phone to herself and started getting dressed. "I'm on my way. And I'm bringing J-Murder. Where you at?"

"I'm at the club. You don't have to come. Stay home. I'll be okay," Syn protested.

"Nah. We don't know when she might hit. Can't take no chances. We have to take this serious. I'm on my way."

"Yes, sir. Roger that," she joked.

"Why the fuck you cracking jokes? This shit is serious. That bitch already showed us how much of a snake she is. Do you got a gun with you?"

"Damn, baby. Calm down. You don't have to be so serious. And yeah, I got my shit with me. I been through too much to leave the house without it."

"Good. Stay put. Here we come. Love you," I said before pocketing the phone.

"Can I come?" Tahiti asked.

"Not this time, baby. I don't know what will happen. Ain't no sense in putting you and the baby at risk. The safest place for you is at home," I told her before going to the gun cabinet and grabbing two Glock .40s.

I found J-Murder in the guest bedroom with the curly blonde-haired police officer. "Sorry, Megan, but I need to steal your boy. Come take a ride with me, my nigga."

When he seen the serious look on my face and serious

tone, he spun to his new flame. "I gotta ride. If I don't make it back before you have to be at work, I'll call you later."

"Are y'all okay?" she asked, eyeing us suspiciously.

"Never been better," I nodded, leaving the room.

"What the move is?" J-Murder asked as we left the house for my BMW.

"Vega lived."

He didn't look surprised. "I tried to find something about the shooting online, but couldn't. I figured she lived because they list all homicides."

"She sent Syn a message that it's on. I'ma need you to stay with her 24/7. This is why I brought you to LA. You gotta be her shadow."

He looked eager to put in work. "You know I got you, my nigga. I never thought I would get paid to be a bodyguard. If I woulda knew I could live in LA in a gated community and get paid to squeeze off, I woulda been doing this shit."

"It's more than one way to make money. You don't always gotta take a nigga shit. I don't know If you remember, but Trigga died protecting Syn. We might be in some shit with heavy hitters. You gotta keep your eyes open, my nigga."

"I'm on top of all of that. I came up under one of the realest niggas that God ever gave breath. I'm certified, Luke. Been settin' niggas on fire since I was a pup."

The Den of Syn had become one of the hottest strip clubs in LA, and that was saying something because there were a lot of gentlemen's clubs in Los Angeles. Athletes, entertainers, moguls, dope boys, and business people flocked to the club every night of the week. And the women were some of the finest in the world – black, white, yellow, Puerto Rican, and Asian.

I looked for Syn on the floor as soon as I walked in. I couldn't find her, but I spotted the manager by the bar. "Hey, Diamond. Where your boss?"

"Hey, Luke. I think she in the back."

I turned to J-Murder, whose eyes had found Fettish's thick ass. "I'ma go in the back. You good up here?"

"Oh, yeah. Got somethin' I need to look into," he grinned.

I found Syncere in the office, sitting at her desk and going through logbooks. "There goes my baby!" I sang.

"Hey, Superman," she smiled, accepting my kiss on the lips. "You smell like Tahiti. It's making my pussy wet."

"Let's go back home and get in bed. Tahiti said something about five orgasms making the baby come out easier. It's on you to give her number three."

She kissed me again. "That girl is crazy. Always making up shit. But I got that. I just have to finish checking this logbook. You're the accountant, so you should look through this book for me."

I grabbed the thick green book. "What are we looking for?"

"I'm looking for MZ Main Attraction's work days last month. She think she can come and go when she wants because she gets requests from the ball players. Bitch don't know who she fucking with. I don't give a damn about her Instagram followers. The Den of Syn makes stars, not the other way around."

It took about twenty minutes to help Syn find what she was looking for. When we walked back out onto the floor, I paused to look for J-Murder. He wasn't with Fettish. Then my phone rang. It was the man of the hour.

"Where you at? We ready to go."

"I'm still here. At the table by the bar, but don't look at me. It's some Crip niggas in here asking about Syncere. Four tables away, on your right."

I looked out of the corner of my eye. They were easy to spot. Three of them dressed in their colors, not hiding the fact they were eyeing me and my girl. "I see 'em."

"But that ain't it. On yo' left is two niggas wearing suits. They just started watching y'all. And they jackets bulky on the sides."

I pulled Syn close, acting like I was telling her something private, casually looking to the left. I spotted the niggas wearing dark colored business suits. They laughed, acting as if they weren't watching us.

"What's going on, baby?" Syncere asked.

"Okay, Murder. We about to walk out. Watch our backs." After hanging up, I filled Syn in. "The Crips on our right and the niggas in suits on our left watching us. Let's get outta here. J-Murder gon' watch our backs."

I watched the Crips out of the corner of my eye as we passed. They were reckless young niggas, itching for an opportunity to kill somebody, and they didn't care when or where they put in work. As we passed, they stood and reached for their waists. All of them had black semiautomatic pistols.

I pushed Syn behind a table and pulled my Glock. The gang members let loose with their cannons, all hell breaking loose in the club. Good thing they couldn't aim, because they had the drop on me, and I should've been dead. Instead, I ducked behind a booth and let my Glock do the talking. I didn't know if I hit anybody. I just wanted to get them off our ass.

Syn was at the table next to me firing shots while staying hidden. Out of the corner of my eye I noticed the niggas in suits. Everyone in the club panicked, ducked, and ran except them. They just got low and watched. Something told me they were pros. Then they pulled out what looked like space guns.

I kicked off the booth, sliding on my back to get closer to Syncere and out of the space guns' line of sight. Then I watched as the niggas in suits turned their guns on the Crips.

Their machine guns sounded like thunder. Terrible thunder. And when the bullets hit the Crips, their bodies seemed to explode as limbs and chunks of flesh flew. Two Crips went down. I had never witnessed that kind of destruction, and it had me scared to move.

Shooting from behind the men in suits got their attention. J-Murder was letting them have it. He hit one of them in the head, dropping him forever. The other one took a couple bullets to the upper body, not even flinching. Then he turned the space gun on J-Murder and sent exploding bullets at the Trigga Klan goon. I didn't know if my li'l nigga got hit because the bullets exploded in the bar, wall, and whatever else they hit, sending debris flying all over.

Instead of trying to help his friend, the sole survivor in the suit grabbed his fallen comrade's gun and let them wreak havoc while he backed out the door. I stayed my ass on the floor next to Syn and let him go. No way I was getting into a shootout with a nigga who had a gun that shot bombs.

Everything went quiet for a couple seconds before I heard movement again. The last surviving Crip ran for the door. I pointed the Glock at him and squeezed. And missed.

"Luke! Syn! Y'all a'ight?" J-Murder called.

I helped Syn stand up. "Yeah. We good."

"Awe, shit," she mumbled as we looked around.

The club looked like someone had thrown grenades inside. Giant holes were in the walls, still smoking. Tables and booths were destroyed. Bodies lay all over the floor, most of them still alive, but the dead ones were ugly sights. The Crips' blood and body parts were mixed together like someone had thrown two life-sized Mr. Potato Heads on the floor, scattering all the parts. On the other side of the room was the nigga in the suit. Blood leaked from a single gunshot wound to the back of his head.

And that's when the club-goers seemed to wake up. Screams filled the air as people got up and ran for the exits.

J-Blunt

Chapter 14

Syn

"I just told you, I don't know anything about the shooters. I don't know anybody affiliated with the Crips. I'm from Wisconsin. I just moved to LA. And I don't know the man in the suit, either. I'm pissed they shot up my damn club. Who's going to pay for all the damage? Oh, yeah. Me," I vented, rolling my eyes at the pair of white men wearing tacky suits that insisted on questioning me again.

"Ma'am, anything you can tell us about the shooters would help. Some witnesses say the man in the suit had a space gun. Is this accurate? What did you see?"

"I didn't see any guns. I was too busy hiding and trying to stay alive. All I know is they fucked up my club."

"I've never seen that kind of ammo or shell casings," Detective Alison said.

"These guns don't exist, and they were in your club. This is why we are speaking to you again. This is very important, Miss Evans. We need to know what you know."

"And I'm telling y'all again that I don't know shit. I was on the floor with everyone else."

"Why were they trying to kill you?" Detective Jones asked.

Me and the veteran cop had a long stare. "I don't know what you're talking about. I thought y'all said they were shooting at each other."

He looked at me like I was prey. "Witnesses say the gangbangers were asking about you. Were the guys in suits protecting you? And why weren't your cameras recording that night? A club like yours, one of the hottest in LA, doesn't have security cameras on? Sounds kind off suspicious, and I ain't buying."

The detective obviously didn't know who he was fucking with. I don't fold under pressure. I'm a diamond. Pressure makes me shine brighter. "What you're buying is not my concern. This ain't a store, and you're not a customer. I'm a businesswoman, and I don't appreciate being treated like a criminal. I told you I was on the floor trying to survive. And I'm sorry my security system went down and doesn't meet your standards. Your police work doesn't meet mine. Stop shooting and locking up black people and you might get better results."

The stares from the homicide detectives were hard. I had pissed them off. Good. Now I hoped they would get the hint and leave me alone.

"Okay. You want to play that game?" Alison asked. "Let me tell you something, Loretta. We know about you and Luke Swanson's drama in Wisconsin. Both of you did time in prison for murder. Now it appears your bullshit had followed you to our city. But you know the difference between us and those farmers you call cops in the beer and cheese state? We don't fuck around. We have more money and more resources. And you've just been added to my shit list."

"A place you don't want to be," Jones laughed.

"Well, if neither of you have any more questions, you can leave. Next time you want to talk, call my lawyer."

The cops stood slowly, wearing mean mugs. Jones spoke. "We'll leave, but I have one more question. You're a convicted felon. Witnesses say they seen you shooting a gun. Where is it, and why didn't you tell us you were firing a weapon?"

"Because I didn't. Like you said, I'm a felon. I can't own a gun. Have a good day, gentlemen."

"Wait. I also have another question," Alison said. "How long have you been using?"

I looked at him like he had just offered me a hit of LSD.

"What the fuck are you talking about?"

"Your eyes. You got crazy pupils. What kind of pills are you taking?"

"Get out of my house!"

When the police left, I fell onto the couch and let out a long, frustrated breath. Four days had passed since the shooting at my club, and I still had no idea why the Crips were looking for me or who the niggas in suits were. The girls at the club hadn't heard anything, either, which was why I was staying in the house. People wanted me dead. Obvious signs pointed to Reign and Vega. Had they both hired goons to take me out? And what were the chances their hired goons would try to kill me on the same day and end up shooting each other?

"Damn, Syn! That was some boss ass shit!" J-Murder smiled, walking over to look out the window. "I never heard nobody give it to they fag asses like that. You a beast, shawty. Now I see why Luke made that choice."

I ran a hand through my hair. "They know I have money to buy good lawyers. Police abuse the poor because they don't have a voice. And what do you mean, Luke made a choice? What choice?"

He sat on the couch across from me. "When we was cellies in the county jail, I asked him why he didn't stop fucking with you after he got the pass from Calico. In so many words, he said he loved you and you was his girl. He was riding with you. Now I see why he couldn't walk away. You a boss."

Hearing the words touched me. It felt good to know that Luke thought highly of me even when I was the cause of all his legal problems. It made me smile. "Get it right, li'l nigga. I'm a Boss Bitch."

"Right. Boss Bitch," he laughed. "I heard some of the shit they said while I was hiding. Do you think they will be able to get that footage?"

"It's already destroyed, baby boy. Nobody can get it. I can't let them see you killing somebody. You are family, and we not gon' let them get their hands on you. You still a baby. Got your whole life ahead of you."

"Stop playin', Syncere. I ain't no baby. I'm a gangsta."

"You know what I meant, nigga. I mean you're young. Still have a lot of living to do."

"You sound like my moms," he laughed.

The words felt like a punch to the chest. They reminded me that I used to be a mother, and I had killed my only child. As I stared into J-Murder's youthful face, I found myself wanting to protect him, give him the opportunity to be something other than a street nigga. "How old are you?"

"Just turned twenty-three," he said proudly.

"Is this the only thing you want to do with your life? Be a shooter?"

"Shit, this all I really know, you know? I quit school in middle school. I been poppin' niggas since I was a shorty."

"But don't you want more out of life? Trigga died trying to protect me, and I don't want the same thing to happen to you."

He looked away, taking a moment to reflect. "I'm good, Syn. Real shit. The streets is in me, and I know I'ma die in 'em. The G on my gangsta can't be erased."

"I can tell you fucked with Trigga. He said something similar when he died. He was a beast. I seen him crush two or three people right before they shot him. He was a real nigga."

"The realest. But can we get off this soft-ass shit. I ain't one of them emotional niggas. I wanna know how we gon' move on them Crips and them niggas in suits."

"I don't know yet. I haven't heard anything. But I don't want to see them guns ever again. I ain't never seen no shit like that in my life. It was blowing them niggas' bodies apart."

"Was like they bullets had bombs in 'em. I want one of them. They make Dracos look like twenty-twos."

"I know," I agreed. "That's scary."

"I think Vega sent the Crips and Reign sent the niggas in suits. Them showing up at the same time was a coincidence."

"I think the same thing. And I don't know how to get to either one of they asses. Which got me back to square one. We have to wait."

***

"I don't like what happened with the police. Why couldn't you just play the scared, innocent woman role? Damsel in distress? Why you have to turn up and fuck with them?" Luke asked.

"Because they were talking to me like I was a weak-ass bitch. Like I didn't know better. I didn't like that shit. They knew our pasts. They knew I knew more than I said. They tried to squeeze me, and I let they ass know I wasn't a punk-ass bitch."

"C'mon, baby. This ain't no ego trip shit. This real life. The feds about to get involved because of them damn guns. They won't care about them dead niggas killing each other. They'll comb through our entire lives and put cases on us just to get us to tell some other shit. You see what they did to Trump lawyer. The feds don't fuck around."

I took my eyes off the road to mug his ass. "You don't think I've thought about this? And even if the feds do come, I ain't telling they ass shit, either. This is not about my ego. This is about standing on my principles and taking care of my people. If I would've gave them the security footage, J-Murder would be in jail right now facing charges. I know you didn't want that."

He got mad. "Quit playing, Syn. You know I ain't saying

that shit. I didn't want the police added to our list of enemies, but it might be too late for that. I thought we came to LA for a new start, not to get involved in more shit. Got Crips and niggas with vaporizing guns shooting at us. I'm tired of this shit!"

Silence filled the Range Rover. We were headed to the modeling agency so I could get some papers to work from home. Plus, I wanted some air. I had been holed up in the house for four days and was going stir-crazy. The only way I could leave the house was with Luke by my side, but now that we were out and about and arguing, I wasn't so sure if I should've brought him with me.

"You don't have to come in with me," I told him after I parked.

He gave me a look. "Stop playing. Just because we had a disagreement don't mean I'ma neglect my responsibilities. If anybody want to get to you, they have to go through me first."

Even though I was mad at him for questioning my handling of the police, hearing the love in his voice softened me up a little bit. "I know this is not what we wanted, baby. I'm tired of this drama, too. I was hoping to come to LA and eat Tahiti's pussy and suck your dick until I was old, but it don't seem like that's a part of God's plan for us right now. But I promise I would rather go through all this bullshit with you by my side than have a peaceful life with another man. I love you, I'm in love with you, and I need you. And I will do whatever to make sure we survive this."

He stared at me for a moment. "I'm in this, babe. All the way. 'Til death do us part. Nothing will ever change that. Not the feds, not space guns, not Reign, Vega, or Crips. You are my everything, and I'm not going nowhere. I love you."

After sharing a make-up kiss, we hopped out of the SUV and went into the studio to grab the papers I needed. On the way out, I stopped to lock the door when something caught my attention. It was a little past 10:00 PM on a clear summer night. The streetlights reflected off a black Dodge station wagon parked across the street. I remembered seeing it when I left the house, parked just beyond the gate that fenced in our neighborhood. Now it was parked across the street from my modeling agency. I didn't believe in coincidences.

"Don't act like you notice, but that black station wagon followed us from home," I whispered to Luke, keeping a hand in my purse as we walked toward the Range Rover.

"I see them. I'm not getting in the car until you start it up. I'ma stay ready."

I tried to look in the car as I climbed in the truck. I couldn't see a thing because the windows were tinted. Luke pulled his pistol, concealing it by his side as he stood outside the truck. After I started the engine and put the truck in gear, he got in.

"Looks like it's three niggas in the car. I think it's them Crip niggas again. They reckless, so shit might go down any moment."

I pulled the Glock from my purse, setting it in my lap as I drove through traffic. The Dodge followed, staying a few cars behind. Luke watched the side mirror intently, clutching his pistol, ready to shoot. I thought of the man he used to be and who he was now. They were night and day. The man in the Rover's passenger seat was trained and ready to go, and I loved that nigga because he did it for me.

"I'm not going back home. What do you want me to do?"

He was quiet for a few moments. "You remember the spot where we fucked in the Bentley we rented?" he asked.

I would never forget riding Luke in the backseat of the Bentley. The construction site would be dark and empty. The perfect spot for an ambush.

"I like the way you think, but there is a car full of niggas. How do we get them?"

"Element of surprise. They not expecting us to go on offense. Gimme your gun. I'ma get 'em by myself."

I didn't even get the chance to protest before he took my pistol. The drive to the construction site was tense. I was nervous as hell and expected them to start shooting at any moment, but they didn't. They remained a car or two behind until it was only us and the station wagon on the road.

"Pull over right now!" Luke ordered.

I hit the brakes and turned the steering wheel, bringing the truck to a quick, unexpected stop. Luke hopped out with both guns blazing. I watched out the back window as fire sparked from the barrels.

The Dodge sped past, losing control as Luke shot it up. A half block later, the station wagon crashed into a light pole.

Instead of getting in the truck, Luke ran toward the wrecked car. I pulled up behind him as he snatched open the Dodge's back door and pulled someone out. He was a little man with wild dreadlocks. Luke pointed a pistol in his face and shouted threats. The man put his hands in the air, wanting to cooperate. Luke dragged him to the Range and they got in the backseat.

"What the fuck are you doing, baby?" I panicked.

"Drive, Syn! Drive!" he yelled.

I sped away, wondering why the fuck Luke had a hostage in the backseat. Our captive looked terrified. And he was just a kid. He didn't even have a mustache.

"Who the fuck sent you, nigga?" Luke demanded, pointing a pistol in his face.

"I-I don't know, cuz. I'm just a shooter. I-I take orders."

"What's yo' name, li'l nigga?"

"D-Deville."

"What set you with, Deville? Who sent you?"

"C'mon, cuz. You know I can't tell you that. Dem niggas gon' whack me, cuz."

"I'ma whack yo' ass if you don't tell me who the fuck sent you, nigga!"

The youngster grew quiet, like he was thinking about telling us. Luke put the pistol to his head.

"Wait!" I yelled, stopping him from killing the boy. "Tell us something, baby boy. Give us a name or phone number. I don't want you to die. Don't be stupid. Save yourself. I'll give you ten thousand dollars if you tell us something. Just call them so we can talk."

The money got his attention, but he was still skeptical. "Ten Gs just so you can talk?"

Luke lowered the gun. "Yeah, li'l nigga. Take the money. Name and number."

"Um. When am I gon' get the money? How I know y'all ain't gon' fuck me over?"

"You don't, li'l nigga!" Luke yelled, showing the pistol again. "I could still kill yo' ass. Give us the muthafuckin' information!"

"He won't shoot you," I cut in. "You know who I am. I own a strip club and modeling agency. I don't have the money on me, but you'll get it before the night is over. Right now we need you to call your people so we can try to stop them from killing us."

He let out a heavy breath. "His name is Fats. He our OG. 687-5341."

Luke called on speakerphone. "What it do?" a deep voice answered.

"This Fats?" Luke asked.

"Yeah. Who dis?"

"This Luke. I'm sitting here with your boy, Deville. Why you want us dead?"

The line went silent for a few moments, then Fats laughed. "Who the fuck is this playin' on my phone? Bitch-ass nigga, this shit ain't funny!"

Luke pointed the gun at the young gunner. "Tell him I ain't playing."

"This ain't no game, OG. They fucked up Reno and Tree. Caught us slippin' and snatched me up."

"What the fuck you give these muthafuckas my numba for, fool-ass nigga?"

"'Cause he don't want to die," I spoke up. "This is Syncere. Tell me why you're trying to kill me. I don't know you, do I?"

"You fucked with the wrong people, Syncere. They was under my protection. Eye for an eye."

"What the fuck are you talking about? I don't know your people. Who are they?"

"You tried to smoke my homegirl, Vega. This a clap-back."

"Let's talk about this," Luke cut in. "We got money. How much will it cost to end this?"

Fats was silent. "Okay. I'm a businessman. I'll listen. But I don't talk on the phones. Come see me."

Chapter 15

Luke

Instead of taking Syn with me to meet Fats, I took J-Murder. She was the target, and I couldn't risk bringing her into the lion's den. She was my insurance policy. If I didn't make it out alive, she would tell the police about Fats and our conversation. Or, knowing Syncere, she'd try to hunt him down and kill him.

The meet was at a trap house in a south central neighborhood under the Crips' control. If Fats wanted me dead, I wouldn't make it out of the neighborhood. And I was okay with that, because I was going to take a bunch of Crips with me. I held two grenades in the front pocket of my hoodie, and so did J-Murder. If shit got ugly, I was going to turn their hood into a warzone.

We followed Deville up the walkway of a blue and black painted house where four Crips stood on the porch smoking weed and drinking beer. They all held guns in plain sight, mugging me and J-Murder as we approached. When I walked up on the porch, a big nigga with wild hair and a long, braided beard stepped to me, clutching a pistol tight in his grip.

"I'll bang yo' ass, Loc! You lucky," he mugged.

I didn't respond, just stared him in his eyes, keeping my hands in my pocket and squeezing the levers on the grenades, loosening the pins. I was ready to die, but I didn't think he was.

After a stare-down, Deville led us into the house. More Crips were lounged around the living room, smoking weed and watching a basketball game. When we walked into the living room, all eyes were on us.

"Which one of y'all is Luke?" a big nigga with blue shoulder-length dreads asked.

I nodded. "I am."

He gave me a once-over before standing and grabbing a chrome .44 Magnum from the table. I pulled the pin from one of the grenades, ready to light us up.

"I'm Fats. This is my family," he introduced. "But this li'l nigga right here is no longer part of the family."

Before Deville could say a word, Fats lifted the hand cannon and blew his face apart. I was ready to drop the grenades on the floor and blow shit up, but Fats lowered the pistol.

"Nardo, D-Bo, y'all clean this nigga up. Luke, you and yo' boy come to the kitchen so we can talk business."

I looked to J-Murder to make sure he was okay. He nodded, seemingly un-phased by the execution. After giving Deville's spasming body one last look, we followed the OG into the kitchen.

Fats sat the big revolver on the table, pointing it at me as we had seats. Then we had a long stare. "Tree called me. You killed Reno. Shot up Tree, but he gon' live. Stacks and G-Ball got killed by some niggas in yo' girl club with machine guns. Not to mention Deville's brains on the living room floor. You fucked up five of my family members, Luke. Tell me why I should let you leave this house?"

I pushed the pin back into the grenade in my front pocket while thinking of the appropriate response. "Because you are a business man, Fats. And so am I. I'm an accountant by day. I came to talk business, not die. I got a baby on the way, and I would like to be around to raise it."

Fats smiled. "Cool under pressure, huh? I like that about you, Loc. You didn't even flinch when I blazed Deville. You ain't no lame, huh?"

The question was rhetorical, so I didn't answer. Instead I focused on why I was here. "So, what are we going to do to solve this conflict? Did Vega pay for our heads?"

Fats leveled his stare. "She paid for your girl. Twenty-five racks. So I'ma start the price of peace at fifty. Plus twenty-five Gs for each injury or loss suffered to my family as a result of fucking with you and your girl. That puts us at one hunnit seventy-five thousand."

"One hundred," I countered.

He laughed. "This ain't negotiable, Luke. You agree to these terms or you don't leave this house."

I glanced at J-Murder. He looked like he wanted to use his grenades, but I didn't want to go out like that, so I pulled both grenades from my pocket, keeping them in my fists as I rested my arms on the table. J-Murder did the same.

Fats' eyes grew wide at the sight of the explosives.

"To be honest, my nigga, I didn't think you would let me leave this house alive. So, we brought life insurance. If I wasn't leaving this house alive, wherever I went, I was taking you with me. I don't wanna die, Fats. I got a baby on the way, and I haven't even turned thirty yet. Plus, I gotta find out who them other niggas was at the club with the space guns that tried to kill us. So, my counter offer is one hundred Gs and these two grenades. In return, I want you to be my eyes and ears in the streets. You see something, say something. I will hit your pockets every time. Also, I need Vega's information. That bitch snaked me for the last time, and she gotta go. I'll throw in an extra twenty-five for that. Can we agree to this peace treaty so I can get back to living my life?"

After another stare-down, Fats spoke. "As a chess player, I can appreciate a good counter move. If you don't play chess, you need to, 'cause you got hella game. I accept the terms of the agreement, Luke. I got twins at home, and they daddy's boys. Daddy needs to make it back home. When do I get my money?"

"I'll have it tomorrow. Every dollar. Give me Vega's information when I give you the money. And you can keep these," I said, leaving the grenades on the table as I stood.

***

I made good on my word to get Fats the money, and he made good with Vega's address. My next task, before killing Vega, was to convince Syn to let me take care of everything.

When I walked in the house, I was mobbed by my women, Syncere on one side, Tahiti on the other.

"Oh, I'm so glad you made it back! We were so worried," Syn said, pulling me in for a kiss.

"Is it over now? Can we go back to normal?" Tahiti asked.

"Yeah. We good. Fats on the team now."

"I gotta know what it feel like to have two dimes fighting for my attention when I walk in the house," J-Murder laughed.

"We're not fighting," Syn said.

"We're sharing," Tahiti said.

"And sharing is caring," I added.

"You think Derikka would get down with me and Megan?" he asked.

Syn frowned. "My assistant, Derikka?"

J-Murder nodded, a lustful look on his face. "Yeah. When you gon' hook a nigga up?"

She waved him off. "No, J-Murder. She is a good girl and I don't want you fucking my assistant."

"C'mon, Syn. You know good girls be the freakiest ones."

"Nah, nigga. I'm not playing, either. Don't fuck my assistant. For real."

"Dang, man," he pouted. "Why you gotta ruin a nigga fantasy?"

"Why don't you get some girls from the club? They like your bad ass," Tahiti offered.

"'Cause they ain't good girls. But don't trip. MZ Main

Attraction been trynna slide in my lane. Since you acting funny with Derikka, I'ma train her to be my bottom bitch. Show y'all that Milwaukee niggas got pimp shit in our blood," he said before walking to the kitchen.

"Your guy is crazy," Syncere laughed.

"I already know. But listen, baby, we need to talk."

She frowned. "Okay. But why you sound so serious?"

"'Cause it is serious. I need you and Tahiti to go to Wisconsin. To the house in Fox Lake. Stay there until I get rid of Vega."

"Oh, hell nah! You ain't about to make me run from this bitch. I told you I wanted to be the one to kill her. She is my problem. I need to make up for letting her live while I was locked up."

"This not up for debate, baby. You had your shot. Literally. I'ma get this shit over with, and I don't wanna argue about it."

She got mad and raised her voice. "The fuck you don't wanna argue, trynna tell me to leave! This is my problem to finish, and I'm not leaving. Hell nah. No way!"

"Why the fuck you always gotta argue about everything? I told you, I got it. You my bitch, and I'm yo' nigga. If I said I got it, that means I got it. We don't have to debate every decision. Pack yo' shit and leave."

Fires blazed behind her cinnamon-brown eyes, her nostrils flaring, chest heaving. "Don't talk to me like I'm a weak-ass bitch, 'cause I'm not. You knew how I was when you met me. I speak my mind and take care of my own business. I'm a boss, nigga."

I leveled with her. "Am I your man or not?"

"What that got to do with anything?"

"Just answer the question. Yes or no? Am I yo' nigga?"

She mugged me. "You know you is."

"Didn't I take care of Calico and all the bodies in the

127

warehouse? Didn't I risk everything for you and put it all on the line? If I say I got it, let me do it. Go to Fox Lake. I got it."

We had a long, will-testing stare-down, neither of us wanting to give in. But when it came to challenging me, she would always back down first. This time being the exception, because my phone rang. It was Travis.

"What's up brother?"

"Luke! DEFCON one, bro! I need you to get over here."

I heard panic in his voice. This was serious. "What's going on, bro?"

"Stupid-ass trade war with China is fucking with the stocks. We told Milton to invest in Harley Davidson, and the stocks just plummeted. We lost thirty million!"

It felt like I had been punched in the stomach. Milton Braggard was our most valued and richest client. "Shit. This is fucked up. I can't deal with this right now. I have an important move to make here at home."

He got hysterical. "What could be more important than our firm right now? We have to figure this out before we lose all of our clients. We could lose the firm."

I couldn't tell him I had a date with a bitch I needed to kill. I also didn't want to let our business go down the drain. "I got too much heat on me right now. Serious shit I need to handle. I want to be there, but I can't right now."

"What? Are you fucking serious? Did you just hear what I said? Milton is going to blow a fuse when he hears we lost thirty mil. I'm not taking the wrap by myself. You've been half-assing this whole week. What the fuck, bro?"

That shit pissed me off. "Do I really gotta explain this shit to you, nigga? You know what I'm going through. Our club just got shot up. We almost got killed. My life and the life if my family is more important than Milton's money. Fuck you talking about?"

"So, that's how it is, brother? We're really doing this? You turning your back on the firm?"

Talking to this nigga was making my head hurt. But he was right. I couldn't turn my back on the firm. It was my dream. "C'mon, man. You know I'm not turning my back on the firm. Why would I give up on something I helped create? I'm dealing with a lot, nigga. Like trying to stay alive. If I'm not breathing, you'll have to deal with everything on your own. Let me take care of my family. When I put this shit behind, I'll be back with the firm. One hundred percent."

"Don't worry about it, Luke. I got it. Do what you have to do."

The tone of his voice let me know the words were forced. I had never known how much of a bitch he was until now. "Fuck. I'm on my way."

"Where you going?" Syn asked.

"We just lost thirty million dollars. Trav is acting like a bitch. I gotta go to the firm. But you still need to pack. Go to Fox Lake."

She walked toward me, fires still blazing in her eyes. "You lucky I love your ass, nigga. Give me a kiss."

I leaned down, expecting a peck on the lips. She grabbed my face and kissed me aggressively, biting the shit out of my bottom lip.

"What the fuck is wrong with you?" I yelled, checking my lip for blood. Sure enough, I was bleeding.

"That's for treating me like a basic bitch," she smiled. "I'm a boss."

***

I took J-Murder to the firm with me and had him wait in the car. I had been on edge since the niggas in suits shot up the club. so I made sure to keep a heat on me. I had also limited my time at the firm. I didn't want Travis or any of our clients to get caught in a shootout.

When I walked in the conference room, Travis sat in front of the TVs. We had six thirty-two-inch monitors on the wall. All of them were turned on stations related to the stock market.

"What you got, man?"

He spun to face me, aged by stress, anger in his eyes. "This is some bullshit, Luke! The stocks keep dropping. Everyone looks to be selling. We've lost too much to pull the plug. But I'm not sure if it'll rebound."

I studied the information scrolling across the screens. Investors had panicked and either cashed in or sold their stock in Harley. Our shares had dipped from forty million to ten. The trade war on aluminum was affecting our business, and there wasn't a damn thing we could do about it.

"Damn, Travis. This is fucked up, and I'm not sure if we can do anything. Cash out and buy ten mil of a stock that is on the rise."

He gave me a disappointed look. "C'mon, Luke. People who don't know anything about investing can come up with that answer. That's not a good enough solution. We need a sure thing. A power move. C'mon, nigga. You've been around me for six years. I know you have something better than that."

Truth was, I didn't have a better answer. Most of my focus was on staying alive and killing Vega without going to prison. "I don't know, Trav. My head ain't fully in the game. Niggas is trynna kill me and my girl. Staying alive is all I can think about."

"Yeah. I thought about that after you hung up. This is fucked up. What did the police say? They find anybody?"

"Nah. They think we know who did it. We've gone from victims to suspects."

"Damn. That's fucked up, man. Is that the cost of being black in America? Even when you get shot at, you're still guilty of something."

"Yeah. That's how it looks. We're going to Wisconsin for a couple of days. Try to let things cool off. The only thing I can think of to solve our problem is to tell Milton the truth. Let him know about the loss and reinvest. If he really fucks with us, he'll trust us to get the money back. Not much else we can do."

Trav hung his shoulders. "Yeah. Guess there isn't much we can do. Damn, I wish you didn't have to leave town. How the fuck did you get all this drama in your life, anyway?"

"Shit happens. But I'm gonna get to the bottom of it all soon. And when I put all of this behind me, I'll be back focused on the firm. I just need a little more time."

"Alright, bro. I'll take care of the firm. Take care of yourself."

***

I waited forty-eight hours before making the move on Vega. According to Fats, she and Sofia were holed up in a house in Long Beach. I did a drive-by the day before to familiarize myself with the neighborhood. I figured out the best way for me to get in the house was with the help of the Crip leader, so I had him call and press on her the need to meet face-to-face after losing five of his family members. Only Fats wouldn't show up on her doorstep. It would be me and J-Murder.

After parking in front of the house, we checked the block to make sure there wouldn't be any witnesses. It was almost 11:00 PM, and the block was nearly deserted except for a few late-night stragglers.

"You ready?"

J-Murder smiled at me from the passenger seat. "You already knew that."

I checked the silencer on the untraceable nine-millimeter Beretta I bought from Fats. J-Murder had the identical twin. After I was satisfied the gun was locked and loaded, I called Fats.

"I'm outside right now. Let her know."

"Okay. I'm making the call right now. Make sure you don't miss, otherwise that's gon' be extra."

"You got all the money you getting from me. Don't spend it all on bullshit. Make that call."

After hanging up, we exited the car and walked up the walkway, wearing black and blue clothing, pretending to be Crips. As soon as I stepped on the porch, locks on the door clicked. And then it opened. I recognized Sofia instantly. But she didn't recognize me. Yet. The Crip colors were doing their job. When she opened the screen door, I pointed the silenced pistol in her face.

"You bet not say shit!" I whispered, forcing my way into the house. "Where Vega?"

Terror shown in her eyes when she recognized who I was. And in that moment she realized death had come to get her. She took a breath, preparing to open her mouth and scream a warning. I was ready for that and squeezed the trigger. The hammer on the pistol clapped twice, sending a bullet into her forehead, the other into her eye.

Unfortunately, she was able to let out some of the scream.

"Sofia, you good?" Vega called from the back of the house.

J-Murder had been trained by one of the most vicious killers America had ever birthed. My dead friend Trigga was a beast, and the youngster had his instincts. When Vega's voice sounded, he took off through the house, tracking her down like a bloodhound with a scent of its prey. I gave chase, running down a hallway and into a bedroom.

Clap, clap, clap, clap, clap, clap, clap!

I stepped into the room just in time to see Vega fall to the floor. The gun she never got a chance to fire flew from her grip and slid across the floor.

I walked over to get a closer look. Four bullets had punched through her green silk pajamas, spouting red spots all over her torso.

Just to make sure she didn't survive this time, I shot her in the face twice.

J-Blunt

Chapter 16

Syn

"Oh yeah, baby! Stay right there, Syncere. Stay right there!"

I loved the way Tahiti said my name when we fucked. It tickled my ears and turned me on. I loved the sound of pleasure. Shit got my pussy wet and made me want to go harder. I continued sucking her clit, working two finger in her pussy and one in her ass.

"Yeah, baby. Right there. I'm about to cum. Oh shit, I'm about to cum!"

I lifted my head, replacing my mouth with my thumb on her clit so I could watch her face. Tahiti made the best cum faces, eyes closed, mouth open, face twisted up in ecstasy. I wiggled my thumb across her clit like it was a video game controller while pushing fingers deep inside her ass and pussy.

"Oh shit, baby! Oh, God!" she cried.

My girl came like a water fountain. Clear fluid gushed out of her pussy like pee, wetting my hands and the bed. I was so turned on by her squirting that I began licking my fingers. My baby's juices were so sweet.

"Damn, Syn. That shit felt so good. You got my body tingling," Tahiti moaned.

I crawled up her trembling body to give her a kiss. "Good pussy licker. Now, gimme mines."

I continued crawling up her body and sat my pussy on her face. She got right down to business, licking and sucking my pussy like sex was what she was made for. The eye contact made it extra erotic. I ran my fingers through her hair, staring down into her eyes while she looked up at me. Then I felt her fingers slip across my pussy and use my juices to wet my ass. When she slipped a finger in my back door, a jolt of electricity shot from my feet to my brain.

"Oh yeah, baby! That's it. Suck yo' boss bitch pussy!"

And she did that like a pro. Shit felt so good I wanted to eat her pussy some more, so I switched to the sixty-nine position.

After we both came two more times, we curled up in the bed to chill. "You make me feel so good," Tahiti confessed, rubbing my back. "I never thought I would be in love with a woman."

"Me either. I just wanted to play around with girls, but you are something else."

"You, think Luke is okay?" she asked, a hint of worry in her voice.

I remained strong. "Hell yeah. Him and J-Murder's little bad ass got it. I was more worried about them not coming back from the meet with Fats. Luke is a smart nigga. Shit, probably the smartest man I ever met. He's good."

"How the hell did you meet him, anyway. Tell me the story."

I laughed at the memory. "Let me just tell you that the man he is today is night and day from the nigga I first met. We met at a club. I was about to shoot his college teammate, but he intervened. Came over wearing a purple suit and acting way too cool. Like he just knew I was going to give him my number. So I didn't."

"So, how did he ends up getting your number?"

"Travis used to be my accountant. He ended up getting a new job and said he would hook me up with another accountant. Turned out to be Luke. He was super feeling his self and started talking about destiny and all this shit. After you gave him the lap dance at Trigga's party, the rest is history. Nigga killed niggas and took bullets for me. Went to jail protecting me. That's my nigga."

"Kind of sounds like he was right about destiny. I think

we all suppose to be together.

I gave her words some thought. "I think you might be right."

"I think that should be the baby's name, if it's a girl. Unless you want to go with Trinity."

Hearing my daughter's name felt like a prick to my heart. I was already emotionally vulnerable from cumming and cuddling, and thoughts of my daughter were too much. I rolled away from Tahiti, my mood turning sour. "I don't want to think about Trinity. Stop saying her name."

Tahiti slid up behind me. "C'mon, baby. Don't do that. Don't shut me out."

"I don't want to talk right now. Just leave me alone."

"But not talking about what's bothering you won't help. You need to let it out. You don't have to hold it all inside or carry the burdens alone. That's what me and Luke are here for. We love you and want you to get better. You don't need the pills."

I shrugged her arms off and sat up in bed, grabbing my clothes from the floor. I needed some space. "I just told you I didn't want to talk about it."

"If you don't talk about it or try to stop taking the pills, I'm telling Luke."

That got my attention, and I spun around to mug her. She sat up in bed wearing a serious look, her smug posture pissing me off more than her words. "I don't know who you think you are or who you think you're talking to, but you got me fucked up. Don't try to blackmail me, bitch. If I don't want to talk about something, I won't. And you better not say shit to Luke or I'm fucking you up."

***

"Yeah, Latia! That's that shit right there. White and

purple go good together," I slurred, trying to keep my balance as I stood outside the dressing room.

"You okay, Syncere?" the ten-year-old asked, giving me a concerned look.

"Yeah, baby girl. I'm good," I lied, swaying a little. "Is you good? Betcha them li'l niggas at school gon' go crazy when they see you with this dress on. Have all they li'l asses walking around with hard dicks," I laughed.

Latia gave me another look.

"Syn, will you stop! You can't be talking to her like that. She's only ten," Tahiti lectured.

I waved her off. "These niggas out here don't care she's only ten. Life is real. Real life is a bitch, bitch."

"Why don't you go wait in the car? I'll pay for her stuff."

"Why? Am I embarrassing you? Am I too loud?" I laughed, the Oxycontin and Hennessey buzzing through my body.

"No, you're not embarrassing us. You're embarrassing yourself. You talking really stupid right now. Latia don't need to hear that. You're drunk. Wait for us outside."

I was starting to get tired of Tahiti's mouth. "You betta watch yo' mouth. Only one Boss Bitch in this family. Remember that. Do I sound stupid to you, Latia."

She looked unsure of her response. "You sound like you've been drinking. You're saying things you wouldn't normally say. You don't have a filter right now."

I burst out laughing. "You sound just like yo' daddy! Yeah, I'm a li'l tipsy. But I'm grown. I can do this. But since y'all wanna act all uppity, I'ma wait outside."

I stumbled my way out of Nordstrom and found the rented Lexus truck. After climbing in the passenger seat, I cut on the music and closed my eyes.

"Syn! Syn, wake up."

I opened my eyes and seen Tahiti staring at me. "What?

What happened?"

"Shay wanna talk to you."

I looked around. We were stopped at a red light. "Where she at? What that ugly bitch want?"

"Who you callin' a ugly bitch, bitch?" Shay said angrily, her voice coming through the car speakers.

For a moment I wasn't sure how to respond. I was surprised she was on the phone. But one thing was for sure, I didn't lie when I called her ugly. "Well, if the shoe fits," I laughed.

"You know what? Fuck you, bitch! I bet you won't talk that shit to my face."

I don't know why I found her attitude funny, but I did. I laughed some more. "Okay. I'm sorry, Shay. I didn't know you was on the phone, and I'm a li'l tipsy right now. What did you want?"

"I want you to call me a ugly bitch to my face. That's what I want, bitch."

Her words were no longer funny, and being called another bitch was starting to get to me.

"She said sorry, Mama," Latia spoke up. "She been drinking."

"I don't give a fuck what that bitch drunk. She betta watch her mouth before I snatch that ho teef out!"

I had enough. "I don't got teef, you thotty-ass bitch! I got teeth. Learn how to talk before you start talking shit, bitch. And if you keep talking, I'ma come over there and beat yo' ass!"

She turned up. "I wish you would, ho! Ain't you on yo' way? I'ma be waiting outside, bitch," she said, hanging up before I could get in another word.

"Go by that bitch house right now! I'ma beat her bitch-ass!" I told Tahiti.

"That's where I'm on the way to. We have to drop Latia

off. But you not about to fight her mom. You drunk. Calm down."

"That bitch the one talking shit. I tried to apologize."

"Syncere, can you please not fight my momma?" Latia asked from the backseat.

I looked over my shoulder at the ten-year-old. She wore the same frightened look Trinity had right before I shot her. The vision shook me to the core, sobering me up instantly.

"Okay. I won't fight her. But yo' momma better not try me."

When Tahiti pulled up to the house, Shay was waiting on the front porch, holding a small wooden bat. She was a couple inches shorter than me with dark skin, big lips, and a humongous booty. I don't know what Luke seen in his baby momma, but she was as basic as basic could be.

As soon as the truck stopped, she walked over, talking shit. "Get out the car and say that shit to my face, bitch!" Lucky for me the window was rolled up or she would've been in my face and might've tried to hit me with the bat.

Instead of getting out of the car and snatching her ass, I ignored her and turned to Latia. "I'll FaceTime you later, baby girl. Talk to your mother and calm her down."

She gave a nervous and scared smile. "Okay. Thanks for the dress, Tahiti."

"You're welcome, baby."

When Latia climbed from the backseat, Shay used the opportunity to reach inside and pull the back of my hair. "Yeah, punk-ass bitch! Talk that shit now!"

I know I told Latia I wasn't going to get in her mother's ass, but that was before the bitch put her hands on me. I hit the latch on the door and hopped out the truck like Batman jumping out the Batmobile. Shay was ready for me and swung the Louisville Slugger at my face, trying to take my head off. She ended up hitting me in the side of the neck.

140

It probably hurt, but I was too faded off the liquor and pills to feel it. But I did feel when my fist crashed into her jaw, and I didn't stop at one punch. I laced that bitch with a left, right, left, right combo that would've made Luke proud. Shay stumbled backward and fell to the ground, the little bat flying from her hand.

I wanted to go stomp her ass out, but Latia's screaming cut through my rage. "Stop fighting! *Stop*! *Fighting*!"

Her voice sounded like something out of a scary movie. I paused to look at Luke's daughter. That's when Tahiti grabbed me.

"C'mon, baby. Get in the car before somebody call the police. We gotta go!"

I allowed my girl to pull me to the Lexus, but not before giving Shay some final words. "Don't ever put yo' hands on me again, you basic-ass, nothing-ass bitch! Stay in your place."

I was in the passenger seat, rubbing the lump on my neck when my phone rang. It was Luke. "Hey, baby," I mumbled, my mood sour.

He took one look at my face and frowned. "What's wrong with you?"

"Your punk-ass baby momma just tried me. Bitch hit me with a bat." I grimaced, rubbing my neck. Shit was starting to hurt.

"Shay hit you? Where she at?"

"At home. We just dropped off Latia. Bitch pulled my hair and hit me with a bat."

"She hit you with a bat? For real?"

"Yeah. And I beat that ass. Weak-ass bitch."

He mulled it over for a moment, struggling to process everything. "Where was Latia? What did y'all get into it for?"

"She was right there. I called her an ugly bitch on some playing shit. I apologized, but the bitch got on all that extra shit and put her hands on me."

"Where was Tahiti?"

"I was there, baby," Tahiti spoke up. I spun the phone to face her. "Your baby momma started it and got that ass whooped. Syncere got them hands!" she laughed.

Luke shook his head. "Okay. I'ma talk to Latia. I called to tell you that everything is good. We took care of that. Y'all can come home."

Chapter 17

Syn

Damn, it felt good to get back to a normal life. No more ducking bullets or having to run for my life. No more problems. And most importantly, no more drama. Feelings that had escaped me for a long time crept back into my being. Peace and contentment. Things finally seemed like they were going to be alright.

I stood off to myself near the bar, overlooking my newly-renovated club. It cost ninety thousand dollars to fix everything the space guns had fucked up. A new bar, new walls, and a lot of new furniture.

"I like the remodeling. It looks better than it did the first time."

I looked to my right and seen the torso of a very tall man. After craning my neck to look up, I was staring in the face of Reuben Jakes, a.k.a. RJ, the superstar power forward of the Los Angeles Lakers.

"Hey, RJ. Thanks for coming, man. How are you doing? Enjoying yourself?"

"Fa sho. Even though them gangbanging-ass niggas tried to put a stain on your business, I still rock with the Den of Syn the long way. I'm still here on champagne Fridays."

Getting the support from the pseudo-mayor of LA made me feel good. "Thanks, RJ. Hearing that really means a lot to me."

"Fa sho. You got the sexiest women in the world up in here. No way I'm missing out on this. By the way, if you could send MZ Main Attraction my way, that would be greatly appreciated."

I gave him a wink. "I'll see what I can do."

He flashed his four-year, one hundred twenty million

dollar smile. "Good looking. Me and some of my teammates in VIP."

When RJ walked away, I went to find MZ Main Attraction. And my girl was truly the main attraction. The black and Brazilian goddess was blessed by God with beauty and booty, and niggas cashed out just to be in her presence. I found her at a booth entertaining Miles Walker, a B-list actor that looked like a cross between Trey Songz and Michael B. Jordan. Even though Miles was finer, RJ's money, status, and support made him more attractive. There was no such thing as an ugly millionaire.

"Hey, Miles. I need to steal your girl," I interrupted.

The B-lister looked disappointed when the stripper goddess removed her forty-eight-inch ass from his lap. "C'mon now, Syncere!" he whined.

I ignored his distressed look. "I need my girl. I'll send you somebody else."

"Damn, boss Lady. I had that nigga right where I wanted him. I'm trynna get that nigga to put me in his next movie."

"That nigga ain't Will Smith or Spike Lee. He still in Netflix movies, girl. I got somebody I need you to keep company. Reuben Jakes is here. Take care of him. And take some girls with you for his team."

Her eyes lit up and she began looking around. "RJ is here? Where?"

"In the VIP. Now, ain't you glad I got you away from Mr. Straight-to-Blue Ray?"

"You know you a boss," she smiled before strutting away.

Even though I was happy with my current pregnant girlfriend, I had to watch her ass while she walked away. It bounced like two basketballs.

"Damn, she got a phat ass!" Bryce admired, walking up behind me.

I was happy as hell to see my favorite muscle-bound

security guard. Me and Bryce went way back to my days of owning the Den of Syn in Milwaukee, and he was still the closest thing to a real-life Incredible Hulk I had ever seen. He was only five-foot-ten, but he weighed 250 pounds, all muscle. His shoulders were so big there wasn't any doubt in my mind that he could lift a building. I had flown him and Bone in from Milwaukee to be a part of my club's new armed security team.

"Hey, big man. How's everything going?"

"Good, boss lady. You got top-flight security up in here now. Ain't none of them gangbangin'-ass niggas doin' shit in here again. We got this."

"That's good to hear. Where is Bone?"

"Outside holding down the door. I'm going back out there with him. I just needed to drain the snake. Oh yeah, Luke said to stop by when you get a minute. Him and Tahiti over there."

I followed Bryce's finger. Luke, Tahiti, and J-Murder were at a booth having the time of their lives. There were two strippers in front of them, dancing like they were having an ass-shaking contest. Luke and J-Murder stood and made it rain while Tahiti slapped both women's asses.

"Okay. I'll stop over in a minute. I have to run in the back real quick." I parted ways with Bryce, heading for my office to make a call. Two well-known porn stars were supposed to be the main event, and I wanted to make sure they were still showing up.

On the way to my office, I felt someone watching me. I looked up just in time to see a dark-skinned man in a green, tailored suit look away. Something about him rubbed me the wrong way, but I wasn't sure why, so I paid it no mind and went toward the back, filing the moment away in my mind.

After placing the call and confirming the girls were on their way, I grabbed my purse and pulled out my pills. I hadn't taken any since the afternoon, and now that the business was taken care of, I was ready to get my mind right. After popping two pills, I walked over to the mini-bar to chase them with a drink.

Then the door to my office opened and Tahiti walked in. "What are you doing, Syncere? Get your ass out here and come turn up with us. Karma and Honey out here trynna take Luke home," she laughed.

"I'm on my way out. I had to make a call," I said, eyeing the pill bottle on my desk, hoping she wouldn't notice it.

And that's how I told on myself. Tahiti followed my line of sight to the bottle. "What the fuck, Syn? Is this why you came back here? To get high?" she snapped, grabbing the bottle.

"Don't worry about what the fuck I do. Stay out of my business and give me my shit!"

She put her hands behind her back. "No! You not getting these back. You don't need to be taking this bullshit."

I got pissed off. "You betta stop playing with me. Gimme my shit before I beat yo' ass!"

She got defiant, poking out her chest. "I'm pregnant with your baby, and you gon' hit me over some pills? For real? Well, hit me then, bitch, 'cause I ain't giving you shit! You don't need to be taking this shit."

I wanted to beat her ass, but that would've been wrong, especially over some pills I didn't need to be taking. She was almost six months pregnant with our baby. Hitting her would be bogus, but I wasn't about to let her take my shit, so I snatched her ass up and tried to take my pills back. "Gimme my shit!"

She wrestled with me. "No! Stop, Syn. Let me go!"

"Fuck is y'all doing?"

I turned my head and seen Luke standing in the doorway. Shit. I was caught. So I did the only thing I could do and got angrier.

"This bitch is fucking with me. Get out of my office so I can take care of her."

"It's not me, it's her. She taking pills!" Tahiti snitched.

Luke's face twisted in confusion as he pulled us apart. "Let her go. She pregnant. You gon' fuck around and hurt the baby. And what pills you taking?"

Tahiti tossed him the bottle. "These. She mad because I took them."

I moved to grab the pills from Luke, but was too slow. He held me off with one arm, spinning to read the bottle.

"Why the fuck are you taking Oxycontin?"

I looked away, ashamed to admit my problem.

"She been taking them since Trinity died," Tahiti said. "I've been trying to get her to stop."

I mugged her, really wishing she wasn't pregnant. I wanted to beat her ass!

"Why the fuck am I just now finding out about this? How long have you been taking these pills?" Luke asked, scolding me like I was Latia.

I didn't want to cry. I didn't even know why I was crying, but the tears came. "Because I want to. Because I'm grown. Because I can do what I want. Now, give me my shit back and get outta my office."

"I'm not giving you shit, and I'm not going nowhere. Tell me why the fuck you taking these pills."

I didn't answer. Instead I walked over to the mini-bar and poured a drink.

"She using the pills to stop thinking about Trinity." Tahiti answered for me. "I tried to talk to her about it –"

I threw my drink at her, trying to bust her face open with the glass, but missed. "Get the fuck outta my club, bitch!" I snapped, charging at her. I didn't care if she was pregnant, I was about to beat her ass!

But Luke wasn't having it. He grabbed me around the

waist and held me. "What the fuck you doing? Calm down."

"No!" I screamed, struggling to get free. "I don't want her in my shit. Get the fuck out! You can't hold me forever. When you let me go, I'm beating her ass!"

"Go out on the floor, Tahiti. We'll be out in a minute."

She gave me a mug before leaving. Luke locked the door and sat the pill bottle on my desk.

"What the fuck is this about? Talk."

I ran my fingers through my hair and let out a long breath. "I don't want to talk about it. I don't want to get emotional. This is my club's reopening and I just want to make it through the night. I have guests to entertain. I can't do this right now."

He gave me a long stare. "Okay. I'll tell you what. We don't have to talk about this right now if you agree to talk to me about it after the club closes."

"No, Luke. I don't want to talk about it, period. I'm good."

"No, you're not. And we're not leaving this office until we come to an agreement. I have all night. You don't."

We had an angry stare-down. He wasn't going to let me leave the office, not until I talked or agreed to talk later. "Okay. We'll talk later. That's my word. But I want Tahiti out of my club right now 'cause if I see her, I swear to God I'm busting her in her shit."

"Tahiti didn't do nothing wrong, but I'll take her home because I don't want your night ruined any more than it already has been. And I'm taking these with me. You're done with this shit."

After he pocketed my pills, I straightened up my face and we left the office. As soon as we hit the floor, I could feel eyes upon me. I looked to my left and seen the dark-skinned man in the suit. As soon as we made eye contact, he looked away again. I made it up in my mind to see about him in a few minutes.

148

"Okay, baby. I'ma take Tahiti home. I'll be back," Luke said before going over to Tahiti. They exchanged a few words. Tahiti mugged me before standing and storming outside.

Movement from the dark-skinned man in the suit got my attention. He left the club in a hurry behind Luke and Tahiti. Something about that nigga got to me. It seemed like he was following them.

Then J-Murder walked up. "'Sup with Luke and Tahiti?"

"Some personal shit. She'll be okay. Luke will be back. Did you see that dark-skinned nigga in the green suit that left behind them?"

"Nah, I wasn't paying attention. Too much ass in here to be worried about a nigga rockin' a leprechaun suit," he laughed.

"Something about that nigga rubbed me the wrong way. He was watching me all night, looking away every time we made eye contact. He left as soon as Luke and Tahiti left. It don't feel right."

J-Murder got serious. "Trust yo' gut. Call Luke. Let him know. Too much crazy shit been happening. We gotta be on point for everything."

I took his advice and called Luke. When he didn't answer, I called Tahiti.

"What, bitch?" she answered, heavy on the attitude.

"I don't got time to deal with your bullshit right now. Tell Luke to –"

"Ah!" Tahiti screamed as loud noises sounded in the background.

Taka-taka-taka-taka-taka!

Boom, boom, boom, boom, boom!

My heart sank down into the pit of my stomach as my worst nightmare flashed in my mind. "Tahiti! Tahiti! Luke!"

Nobody answered. And then the call was disconnected.

J-Blunt

Chapter 18

Luke

"I can't believe she on that bullshit, and I'm trying to help her punk-ass. I don't want her to be a dope fiend hooked on pills. She acting like a real bitch. A basic-ass bitch at that. Boss Bitch my ass," Tahiti vented.

"Why didn't you tell me she was on the pills? And Oxycontin, too? This shit like heroin. She might not be able to just quit these cold turkey."

"I wanted to give her a chance to quit on her own or tell you herself. I wanted her to trust and confide in me."

"Keeping it from me wasn't the way to do that. We just went through this with your pregnancy. Now y'all turn around and keeping shit from me. I know what you were trying to do, but you still should've told me. We agreed we was done keeping secrets."

"I know. And I'm sorry. But I don't see how you didn't notice. She was always high and slurring her words."

"Shit, I thought it was from drinking. She killed her only daughter and needed a way to deal with that. Plus, getting high ain't her thing. That's why I never suspected it. But now that I look back, there were a few situations when I knew she was fucked up off more than liquor."

"So, what are we gonna do about this? Did she talk to you about it?"

"No. She wanted to focus on the club reopening. I didn't want to stress her out about it right now. But after the club closes, we'll hash it out."

"Damn, baby. I don't want to go home," Tahiti whined. "I don't want to be in the house by myself. Can't you call and tell her to calm her emotional-ass down? I'm the one that should be upset and emotional. Shit, I'm pregnant."

Headlights in the rearview mirror got my attention. A dark-colored Volvo had followed us from the club and was moving closer to the bumper of the Range Rover. I had been keeping my eye on the car for the last couple blocks. Something about the situation bugged me, so I pulled out my Glock, setting it on my lap.

"Luke, did you hear me? Call her."

"Nah. That won't be a good idea," I mumbled as my phone began to ring. I ignored it, keeping my eyes on the rearview mirror. "I think somebody following us."

Tahiti looked out the back window. "Who is it?"

"That black Volvo. They left the club right after us."

When my phone stopped ringing, Tahiti's rang. "It's Syn," she told me before answering. "What, bitch?"

I slowed down at the stoplight as the Volvo pulled alongside me, craning my neck to see in the car. That's when I seen the pistol hanging out the passenger window. I hit the accelerator and ducked as the bullets began flying.

Taka-taka-taka-taka!

"Ah!" Tahiti screamed.

I hung my pistol out the window, keeping my head low, firing shots blindly at the pursuing vehicle.

Boom, boom, boom, boom!

The windows on the truck shattered as bullets tore into the Range Rover. Tahiti screamed again, grabbing her shoulder.

"You good, baby?"

"No, Luke! I think I got shot. It burns! Look out!"

I looked back to the road just in time to see a car braking about a hundred feet ahead of us. I was going too fast and wouldn't be able to stop. If I crashed, the shooters would finish us off. So I tried to swerve into the next lane.

I ended up clipping the car's bumper. At fifty miles an hour, that was enough to send the truck spinning out of control. After three rotations, the Rover smashed into a car parked at the curb. The whiplash felt like it broke my neck, and the air bags popped, slapping me in the face and dazing me.

A moment later I heard tires screech. The Volvo stopped and two niggas hopped out, rushing the passenger side of the truck while firing semiautomatic handguns. I looked around for my Glock as bullets tore into the truck. It had flown from my hand during the crash, falling in Tahiti's lap. As soon as I grabbed it, Tahiti began screaming, jerking in the seat as bullets tore into her body.

I lifted the Glock toward the shooters and started squeezing the trigger as fast as I could. During the exchange, I could feel bullets piercing my body – my arm, ribs, chest, and neck.

Then my pistol clicked. It was empty.

A second later, tires burned rubber as the Volvo sped away. When I looked toward Tahiti, my heart exploded in my chest. She got the worst of the attack. It seemed like holes covered her entire body. Her face, neck, chest, arms, stomach. The baby!

She gurgled on blood, struggling to breathe. Then she stopped moving.

"No! Tahiti!" I cried, trying to reached out to her, but my arm didn't work. "Tahiti! Baby, wake up!"

J-Blunt

Chapter 19

Syn

"What happened?" J-Murder asked, his eyes wide as full moons.

"I think they just got into a shootout. We gotta go!"

I didn't have to tell the young goon twice. He sprang into action, running toward the front door and leaving me to chase behind him. By the time I got to the door, he was already running across the parking lot to his Camaro.

"What's up, boss lady?" Bone asked when he seen my panicked face.

"I think Luke and Tahiti in trouble," I managed as I ran by. "Tell Diamond to take over for me."

When I got to the parking lot, J-Murder was already in the car, racing toward me. He stopped long enough for me to barely get my butt in the seat before speeding away.

"Where was they going?"

"Home. Just take the normal route. See if we see anything."

I kept my eyes open for signs of the Range Rover as J-Murder sped through traffic. About five minutes later my worst fears came true. A crowd of people stood around with their phones recording. The Rover was smashed against a parked car. My heart sank when I seen all the bullet holes in the frame. There was a body on the ground a few feet away.

"Aw, shit!" J-Murder cursed.

I didn't remember if any words came out of my mouth. All I know is when the Camaro stopped, I hopped out, losing my heels as I ran to the body in the street. It wasn't Luke. There was a gun next to his body, so I guessed he was one of the shooters.

The truck was spun around, facing the opposite direction.

I walked up to the passenger door, feeling like I was going to faint. Tahiti and the baby were gone. Her head was already swelling from the bullets in her face, and her body had so many holes I couldn't count. Blood was everywhere, and her face was slack, devoid of life.

Luke was also covered in blood, head lying against the driver's door. "Luke! Luke!" I called, climbing in the backseat. "Say something, baby. Luke?"

He moaned, mumbling something I couldn't understand, but that was all I needed. "J-Murder, call 911! Hurry up!"

"We already called, ma'am. They're on the way," somebody called.

I climbed onto the center console and grabbed Luke's face, slapping him a couple of times until he opened his eyes. "Luke, wake up, baby! Open your eyes. Stay with me. Please don't die, baby. I won't take the pills no more. I swear to God I won't. Just don't die."

***

The surgery lasted four hours. Luke was shot five times: once in the clavicle, once in the chest, once in the ribs, and twice in the arm. Now he was lying in the hospital bed with tubes coming out of his nose and bandages covering his body. It killed me on the inside to see my nigga fucked up and helpless. I was used to him being strong and fearless. My protector. My Superman. And now he was immobilized. A part of me expected him to get up at any moment and laugh or crack a joke. But I knew that wouldn't happen. It would take time for him to heal.

And then there was Tahiti. She got shot eleven times and died before I got to them. Her and the baby. Their losses added to the holes in my heart and void in my life. And it was all my fault. If I hadn't been a bitch and kicked her out of the club, Luke wouldn't be laid up in the hospital bed and her and the baby would still be alive. This one was on me. It seemed like everyone I had ever loved ended up dying. C-Murder, my daughter, my parents, Rhoda, Jayda, and now Tahiti. I had personally killed three of them myself. Everywhere I went, trouble followed me. And every time I loved somebody, they died. Luke was the exception, but he had been almost killed twice, taking seven bullets because of me. I didn't know how many more times he would put his life on the line for me or how many more shootings he could survive. I wanted all the madness to stop. I needed to find a way to put all of the death and drama behind me.

"How much longer you think he gon' be 'sleep?" J-Murder asked from the small couch near the door.

"They said a few hours. I need him to wake up soon so I can make sure he's okay."

"He good. That nigga got shot damn near as many times as Fifty Cent. I'ma start callin' that nigga Forty Cent," he laughed.

I didn't find the joke funny. I was too worried about my man, and my nerves were too fried to laugh. I wanted a Oxycontin so bad, but I promised I wouldn't take another pill if he lived.

Silence filled the room again, and I continued to sit at Luke's bedside, holding his hand. Then he flinched. I thought I was tripping, so I watched him intently. About thirty seconds later he began to stir.

"Luke? Baby, are you okay?" I cried.

He stirred a little more, letting out a groan before opening his eyes.

"Luke! Oh my god, baby, wake up. I'm right here. Are you okay?"

"I don't know," he groaned. "It hurts all over."

"That's how you know you still alive, nigga," J-Murder

157

smiled, walking over to the bed. "You gotta stop gettin' shot so much, nigga. I'ma start callin' yo' ass Forty Cent."

He laughed, grimaced, and coughed. "Fuck you, nigga. Stop making me laugh. That shit hurt." Then his eyes grew really big, like something scared him. "Where is Tahiti? How is the baby?"

The tears got bigger as they rolled down my face. I couldn't tell him they were gone. It hurt too much. But he read it on my face. I watched the realization and devastation bring tears to his eyes. "They gone?" he asked with a trembling voice.

"They didn't make it, baby. I'm sorry," I cried.

The agony on his face was like he got shot again. He sobbed, big, fat tears dripping down his chin and onto his chest. "Damn! Bitch-ass niggas. I'ma kill all these niggas. That's my word," he promised, trying to get out of bed. But his body wasn't having it, and he collapsed.

"Chill, my nigga," J-Murder said, putting a hand on his chest to steady him. "You fucked up right now. Don't make it worse."

"Stop, baby. He's right. You have to rest. You got shot five times."

"I swear on my dead baby, when I find out who did this shit, I'm killing they whole family," Luke promised.

"Did you see who did it?"

"Nah. They started shooting before I could see faces. But I know it was at least three of them."

"You got one of they bitch-asses," J-Murder said. "He was slumped in the streets when we pulled up."

"I wish I woulda had a longer clip so I coulda got all they bitch-ass."

"You think it was the Crips?"

"Nah. I mean, I can't say for sure, but I don't think so. I think Fats kept his word. But as soon as I get out the hospital,

I'ma find out for sure."

"I don't think it was him, either. He seemed like he was one hunnit. Syn said she seen a nigga in the club wearing a green suit. He left right after y'all did. Can't we get his picture and have my police bitch look at it? See who that nigga is?"

I liked the idea. "That's good shit, baby boy. I'ma text Diamond and tell her to get that footage. You go pick it up and get with your girl."

"Say no more. Hurry up and get better, my nigga. We got shit to do," J-Murder said before leaving the room.

"Where my phone? I need to call my parents."

"I called them already. They're on the way."

He let out a long breath. "How much shit did my momma talk?"

"I don't know. I talked to your dad, but I know she'll have plenty of shit to say when she gets here."

He got quiet for a few moments while I texted Diamond about the security footage. "I think it was Reign," Luke said. "I think he the one that shot up the club with space guns, too."

"We need to find him and put an end to this shit, baby. I'm tired of losing everybody I love to this bullshit. I don't think I can handle another attempt. Damn, I shoulda just gave Calico that money."

"We can't cry over spilled milk, Syn. As soon as I get out the hospital, I'm going to see Barron. We gotta find a way to end this. And I ain't giving them niggas no pleas. They gotta die for killing my seed and Tahiti."

I felt the words as Luke spoke them. Then the room door opened and a Latina nurse walked in.

"Mr. Swanson, I'm glad you're awake. How are you feeling?"

"Everything hurts," he grumbled.

"You're still alive. That's all that's counts. There are some detectives outside. They've been waiting for you to wake up. Do you feel strong enough to talk to them?"

He looked at me. I shrugged, leaving it up to him.

"Yeah. Send them in," he breathed.

"Okay. I'll come back to check on you after they leave. Press the call button if you need anything," she said before leaving.

"Are you sure you want to talk to them?" I asked.

"Nah. But I gotta get it out of the way. You said I hit one of the niggas, right? I gotta give my side of the story for self defense."

When the door opened, Detective Alison and Jones walked in wearing big smiles. I wanted to throw up on their shoes.

"Small fucking world, ain't it?" Alison laughed.

"Looks like whoever shot up the strip club returned for seconds," Jones added.

"What do y'all want?" Luke asked.

"We wanna know who killed the girl and turned you into chopped liver," Jones said.

"Y'all the police. Tell us," I jumped in, not liking the way they were talking and playing around.

"Good seeing you, too, Cookie Lyons," Jones cracked. "Guys, help us get to the bottom of this. What the fuck did you bring to our city? Everywhere you go, dead bodies follow. What's going on?"

"We don't know, man. You get paid to figure this stuff out. You tell me who shot me."

The cops shared an incredulous laugh before Jones began with the questions. "Okay, Swanson. Start from the top. What happened?"

"I'm not sure. I was taking my girl home when somebody pulled alongside me and started shooting. The car looked like a Volvo. I didn't see who they were because I sped off and started shooting back. I crashed and they got out to finish me

160

off. I guess I killed one of them in the process."

"What was the color and year of the Volvo?"

"It was dark colored. Newer model."

"Did you see how many people were in the car?"

"I think there were three of them."

"Where were you coming from?" Alison asked.

"Our strip club. Tonight was the reopening."

"Was it possible you were followed?"

"Maybe. I don't know."

Jones turned to me. "You wouldn't happen to have the footage from last night? Or did you delete it again?"

I wanted to laugh in his face. "Yes. I'll get it for you when I leave."

"Thanks, toots," Alison said before turning back to Luke. "I take it you have paperwork for the gun we found in your car?"

"Yeah. It's registered to me."

"Okay. We'll need to see that. We're going to piece together traffic cam footage along with the witness statements and try to figure this thing out. And after you get well, we'll need a more detailed statement of last night. Unless you want to do it right now?"

I took my cue to leave. "I'm going to get the paperwork for the gun and the security footage. I'll be back soon."

J-Blunt

Chapter 20

Luke

I stayed in the hospital for twelve days. The doctors and nurses wanted to watch my progress because the bullet to my ribs tore up parts of my stomach and kidney. It took a week for me to eat solids again. And when I couldn't take being in the hospital anymore, I put up a fight to get out of there. And it worked. I still had trouble moving my right arm. Bullets ripped through my forearm, bicep, and clavicle. Bone and muscle damage was heavy, so I had to wear a sling. But nothing was going to stop me from getting to the bottom of who ambushed me and Tahiti. They killed my baby. Somebody had to pay for that. And I was starting with Fats.

I had J-Murder do some digging while I was in the hospital, and he was able to find where the gangster lived with his baby momma and twins. And I was about to pay them a visit.

"Who is it?" a woman called from behind the door.

"Luke. Is Fats here?"

"Wait one minute."

"You know we might have to kill this nigga behind this," J-Murder said. "He ain't gon' like us showing up where he lay his head."

"I thought about that. And I don't give a fuck. Somebody killed my baby. I'll make enemies with the whole world to find out who did it."

Movement behind the door got my attention. When it opened, Fats and his long, blue dreadlocks stepped onto the porch wearing a mug that would scare the grim reaper. "Fuck you doin', showin' up at my house, cuz?"

I kept my face hard as stone, not even reacting to his mean mug. "I thought we had a deal, nigga," I accused.

"Fuck you talkin' 'bout, Loc? And how the fuck you find my house?"

I pointed to my right arm in the sling. "I took five bullets and lost my unborn seed. I thought we had a deal, nigga?"

He looked genuinely surprised. "That wasn't me, cuz. On my Cs. I don't know nothin' 'bout that."

We had a brief staring contest in which I tried to detect a hint of lie in his voice or body language.

"Fuck you find my house?" he barked.

I ignored the question for a third time, pulling out my phone and finding the picture of the dark-skinned nigga in the green suit. "You know him?"

Fats studied the picture. "Nah, cuz. That suit-wearing-ass nigga ain't one of mine."

"I figured that. But I had to do my homework. Put your ear to the street and see if you can find out something. I'm paying."

"Send me the picture. I'll see what I can do."

"I will. My bad for showing up unannounced, but I'm playing every card I got and looking under every rock. Somebody gotta pay for this shit."

"Yeah, well, lose my address, nigga. Don't come back through here without calling or I'ma forget about the peace treaty."

We had another stare-off. I understood where he was coming from. I would feel the same way if he showed up at my accounting firm or house. But I also didn't care. Somebody took my seed, and I didn't care who I pissed off trying to find the trigger man. But Instead of expressing my point, I gave a nod before leaving the porch.

"What did he say?" Syncere asked after we climbed back into the car.

"He don't know shit. Mad I came by his house. But fuck that nigga. Let's catch this plane. Get this funeral over with."

***

"The Lord giveth, and the Lord taketh away," the preacher spoke, saying the words as if they would heal the broken hearted. "I know the pain is deep for everyone who loved Tahiti Johnson. She was so young, precious, and full of life. Unfortunately, God had other plans. Just know that her and her baby are in heaven now, being comforted by our Lord and Savior, Jesus Christ. Right now they're smiling down at us, waiting for that magical day when everyone will be reunited in that city with streets paved of gold."

Tahiti's funeral was a sob-fest. Not a dry eye in the house. We had flown her body to Minneapolis to be buried. Since she was shot so many times, the funeral was a closed casket. It was hard for me to remain strong during the long goodbye. I lost my unborn and ride-or-die female. Neither of them could ever be replaced. When they lowered my girl and baby into the ground, it felt like a piece of me got buried with them. And while the preacher said the final goodbye, I prayed for God to help me find who killed my family so I could kill them all.

I left the gravesite with Latia wrapped in one of my arms and Syn wrapped in the other, heading for the car. Ahead of us, my parents walked with Tahiti's mother. My mom tried to comfort the grief-stricken woman to no avail.

After placing Syn in the rental car, I went to pay my final respects to Tahiti's mother and say goodbye to my mom and dad. "Miss Johnson," I called.

Her and my mother spun at the sound of my voice. Tahiti's mother was an older and less attractive version of my girl. The middle-aged woman had black hair and gray eyes, and I could see Tahiti's features in the white woman's face.

"I just wanted to let you know that if you need anything

at all, don't hesitate to call me. I loved your daughter, and I miss her like crazy."

"Is it true?" she asked in an accusing tone, her stare hard.

I wasn't sure how to respond. "I'm sorry, but I don't know what you're talking about."

My mother gave me the eye. "Don't act like you don't know what she's talking about. I told her the truth about her daughter's death. It's all your she-devil's fault. Tell her."

I had never been so pissed off at my moms than I was at that moment. "Why would you tell her that? What the hell is wrong with you?"

"Hold on, boy! Don't talk to your mother like that," Pop warned.

I waved him off. "Y'all need to mind y'all own business and stay out of mine. You didn't have no business saying anything to her, Mom. You wrong for that."

My father stepped closer, getting in my face and pushing me. "Boy, you got one more time to talk to my wife like that and you gon' be in one of these boxes in the ground."

For the briefest moment, I thought about busting my pops in his shit. I was pissed at my mother, and it pissed me off even more that he stood up for her bogusness. "You know she wrong for what she did, Pop. This woman just buried her daughter, and Mom is feeding her nonsense. How you standing up for that?"

Pop was stubborn. "I don't care what she did. She's your mother and my wife, and you gon' show her some respect. I don't care how mad you is or how hurt you is. You know yo' mother is right. You just got shot five times, boy. Yo' arm is in a sling and don't even work. Didn't none of these bullets start flying at you until you started messing with that woman. What the hell is wrong with you? How you smart enough to graduate college, but too stupid to realize Syncere is gon' get you killed?"

Standing face-to-face with my father in the graveyard was the first time in my life I ever seen him come close to crying. Tears welled up in his eyes, threatening to spill. I hadn't realized how my relationship with Syncere affected my parents until that moment. Part of me was still angry at my mom for telling Tahiti's mother that Syn got her killed, and at Pop for backing it up. Another part of me understood their anger and hurt. They wanted to protect me. But I was grown and didn't need their help. I realized that nothing I said would convince them to let me live my life with my woman. So I didn't even try.

I turned away from my father and back to Tahiti's mother. "I'm sorry for your loss. If there is anything I can do, call me."

***

After the funeral, Syn and I hopped a flight to Indiana. We spent the night in a hotel, and first thing the next morning we were sitting in the visiting room at Terre Haute Federal Prison.

When Barron walked in the room, he didn't look happy to see me.

"'Sup, Chief?" I grinned, embracing my big brother with my good arm.

"You," he frowned, looking at my damaged arm. "I don't like seeing you like this, man. It's fucking with me."

"I'm good, brah. It take more than a couple bullets to take me out."

His stare was serious. "All it take is one, nigga."

"Hey, Big Chief," Syncere said weakly, opening her arms for a hug.

He gave her a limp embrace. "'Sup, baby girl?"

After we sat down, he wasted no time getting to the topic

at hand. "Reign sent them hitters at y'all both times. First time it was for Syncere. Second time it was for all three if y'all. I don't know how this nigga getting this information, but he ain't stopping 'til y'all bodied. The nigga is plugged, for real. Mafia or cartel-type shit. They called The Commission. A secret group of heavy-hitters from all over the world that got unlimited reach."

Syn looked devastated. "Shit. What the fuck we get into?"

"Some deep shit. Really, really deep shit," Barron said.

I felt the same as Syn, but I wasn't backing down. "I don't give a fuck who the nigga plugged with. He killed my seed and my girl. I gotta clap back, brah. I can't let this go."

Barron stared at me like I was a stranger he was meeting for the first time. "You don't even sound right saying that shit. But I hear you, li'l bro. I know you can't let it go, especially after losing Tahiti and the baby. So, I got you some help. I know a few niggas in New York that owe me some favors. I'ma call you later and give you the info. Just be careful, nigga. And remember what I said. The nigga is plugged. Don't think he sweet."

"I already know. His niggas shot up the club with guns that had exploding bullets. Got the feds about to get involved."

Barron raised an eyebrow. "What are you talking about?"

"The niggas had machine guns with exploding bullets. I seen 'em blow niggas' limbs off."

"Made my club look like a warzone," Syn added. "Cost almost a hundred thousand dollars to fix."

Barron shook his head. "That shit sound crazy. I'ma put my ear to the streets. The feds gon' get involved if them guns on the black market. Damn, Luke. What the fuck you done got into?"

"I don't know, man. I just wanted to live the good life. They brought this shit to me. I don't give a fuck what kinds of guns the nigga got, or who he plugged in with. I gotta hit back. Plus, he won't stop 'til we dead anyway. I don't got a choice but to make a move."

"Yeah, I know. I just wish I was out," he breathed. "Syncere, will you grab me something to eat? A pop and a pizza would be cool."

"I got you, bro."

As soon as she was out of earshot, Barron got serious. "Why you still fucking with her, nigga? All of this shit is because of that bitch. Fuck wrong with you? Ain't no pussy that good."

"C'mon, man. You sound like Mom and Pops. She my girl. We ride-or-die."

"Fuck that shit!" he exploded. "Mom and Pop right, nigga. This bitch is the devil, nigga. How many times you gotta get shot before you realize that?"

I got upset. "Stop disrespecting my girl. She ain't no bitch. She's my woman."

He let out a long laugh, eyeing me like I was a sucker. "That's how you feel, for real? Ready to lose everybody that love you for a female? You putting your life on the line time and time again 'cause you in love, nigga? You got shot seven times since you been fucking with her, and wasn't none of the beef yours. Ain't that telling you something? She brought all kinds of drama in yo' life and got you shot, but you not mad at her. Yet you get mad at me for calling her a bitch. Stop playing."

"Listen, Barron. She a part of me. She got my back, and I got hers. Yeah, I didn't have no drama in my life before I met her. But she here now. And she ain't going nowhere. Everything we been through made us closer. Our bond is unbreakable. Don't nobody gotta understand that but us. We bonded by blood, love, and war. 'Til death do us part."

Barron looked disgusted. "You sound stupid as fuck,

169

nigga. This ain't no urban romance novel, nigga. This real life. Ain't no pussy worth dying or going to war over. You letting your love for her dull your common sense. Got Mom and Pop worried about you, thinking you gon' die. It sound like you got your mind made up already, but think about our parents. Nigga, they sacrificed everything for you. You was supposed to be the son they could be proud of. And what about Latia? You know that li'l girl need you. So, think about that. Would you rather live for them or die for Syncere?"

The question felt like a punch to the gut. Blinded by my love for Syncere and the need to get revenge for Tahiti and the baby, I forgot about my parents' and Latia's need for me to be alive and well. "Damn, Barron. I don't even know how to respond to that," I admitted.

"You need to think about it, Luke. You're not living for only you, so don't go running toward death thinking it won't affect the people you leave behind. Latia need her daddy, and our parents need a living and free son."

***

"Where are you at, baby?" Syn asked.

I looked away from the TV, having a déjà vu moment when I looked into her eyes. Two years ago we were in the same hotel facing a similar situation. Only that time I had a ghetto pass to escape the drama from Calico. All I had to do was walk away from Syncere. But I didn't. And it cost me time in prison and seven bullet holes in my body. Now I was about to go at a nigga plugged with a secret organization of millionaires that had access to machineguns with exploding bullets.

"I was thinking about Latia. I'm marked for death. If I die, who gon' take care of my baby?"

"C'mon, baby. You can't think like that. We gon' figure

this out. We always do."

"But what if it don't work out that way? You know I love you, baby. And because I love you, I almost got killed. Twice. Barron asked me a question that got me thinking. Do I want to live for Latia or die for you? I couldn't answer the question."

Syn grew quiet for a moment, not knowing how to answer, either. "Damn, baby. I want to be mad that Barron put it to you like that, but I can't be. He's your brother and wants what's best for you. And Latia needs you. She needs you to live for her and help raise her. You wouldn't be wrong for answering that you want to live for her. You're her father. That's what you're supposed to say."

I knew the right answer, so I kept my peace. I needed to live.

Syn rolled on top of me, looking into my face. "Tell me what you want to do and we'll do it. We can take Latia and leave the country. I don't want you to die because of me. We can drop it all right now and leave. Canada, Mexico, Cuba, South America. We can go."

I gave her words some thought. Leaving would be so much easier, but would Reign let us get away and live in peace? If he was connected all over the world, we probably wouldn't be safe until he was dead. And could I live without trying to avenge the deaths of Tahiti and my unborn? "I don't know, baby. It sounds good, but if Reign's really connected, he could reach us anywhere. And I don't like the thought of running from nobody, especially a nigga that killed my seed. I don't think I would be able to let this go without at least making an attempt to get at this nigga."

"Then just let me do it. You don't have to get involved. I'll go to New York and see what I can do."

I gave her a look. "Stop playing, Syncere. Wherever you go, I'll be right there."

"But this is all because of me. I started all of this. Let me go and try to end this. I'm not some weak-ass bitch, Luke. I know how to get down for mine. Since this all started because of me, I should be the one to end it. You're all I have left. I don't have any family, parents, or kids, but you do. If you die, they'll all miss you. Won't nobody miss me if I die."

"You wrong, baby. If you die, I'll miss you. And I don't want to live without you. We're in this together. I got you."

Chapter 21

Syn

I wanted an Oxycontin so bad I could taste it, but I promised to stop taking them if Luke survived. And he did. He was standing next to me, alive and well, as we walked through the airport. It had been two weeks since the last time I got high, and I wanted to ride cloud nine as bad as anything I had ever wanted in my life. But my will to be strong and the need to honor my word meant more than any high I could get from a drug. So I pushed the craving to the back of my head and tried to focus on why we were in New York.

After leaving the terminal, we went to rent a car and headed to the hotel. Thirty minutes later there was a knock on the door. "Who that?" Luke asked, checking the peep hole.

"Kent and Waldo," a deep voice responded from the hall.

When he opened the door, I got my first look at our contacts. Kent was a little man, a few inches shorter than me with dark skin, a bald head, and no facial hair. Waldo was a slim, white man a few inches taller than Luke. He wore sweats and carried a black duffel bag.

"I'm Kent, and this is my partner, Waldo the Russian," Kent introduced. "We got the tools you need for the job."

Waldo dropped the bag on the bed and pulled out the contents: two nine millimeters with silencers, a Mac-12, and a Draco. "You are Luke, no?" he asked in a thick accent, staring at my man's wounded arm.

"Yeah. What's up?"

"You have injured arm? What you plan on doing?"

"Whatever I have to. Reign did this, and I need to return the favor."

Waldo laughed. "Kent, this guy joking, no?"

"Nah, son. You heard. He wanna put Reign in an arm

sling, and we'll help give him the opportunity."

"Who are you two? How y'all connected to this?" I asked.

"Big Chief good friend," Waldo said. "He need favor, I'm there. I owe my life to him. He save me and wife from Mexican cartel. Now I have new life in New York."

"Same here," Kent nodded. "Chief got rid of a fed case for me. An agent had me by the balls, squeezing me. Chief made him and the case disappear. I'm forever indebted."

Hearing their stories and devotion to Barron made me see Luke's big brother in another light. I knew he was a beast, but I never imagined hearing stories about drug cartels and killing federal agents.

"Now that we done with the intros, tell me the plan. How do we get to Reign?" Luke asked.

"Easier said than done, my dude," Kent said. "Mr. Reign is a big deal, brah. You can't just walk up to him and try to take him out. He has security. Real life ex-military. If we are reckless, they will see us coming, and we won't even touch a hair on his head."

"So, what do we do? How do we get to him?" I asked, not wanting to hear we might've traveled halfway across the country for nothing.

"Watch and wait," Waldo said. "Now that you are here, we put heads together and come up with plan. He owns club. *Cinco*. Hottest club in city."

Luke let out a frustrated breath and pulled out his phone. "Alright. We'll get to him before we leave. But what about him? Do y'all know who he is?" He showed them the photo of the man in the green suit from the club.

Waldo studied the picture. "I see him around. Luther. Kent, you know Luther, right?"

The shorter man took the phone. "Yeah. I know this clown. Got a building in Queens. They moving major work outta there. How you know him?"

"He was in LA," Luke said. "He was one of the niggas that put me in this sling."

Waldo smiled. "I always want to know how much money in his building."

***

The full moon lit the block perfectly, allowing us to see Luther's building. It was nicknamed The Matrix. The two-story brick building had eight apartments, all of them controlled by The Gucci Boyz, a drug-dealing clique led by Luther. We were in a minivan parked a half block away. Waldo drove. Luke was the passenger, me in the middle. Kent and J-Murder were in the back. We had been watching The Matrix for about forty-five minutes. Two people stood out front, guarding. People constantly went in and out of the building.

"Y'all see that?" J-Murder pointed.

A tall, light-skinned man left The Matrix, walking toward the minivan.

"Yeah," I nodded. "He went in there a while ago."

"He might be part of the clique. Let's get him. See what he know," Luke said.

"Not right here," Kent spoke up. "They got people out front. Let's get him on the next block."

"Good call," Waldo said, starting the van.

After driving around the block, J-Murder and I got out, planning to head off our vic. Everyone else stayed in the van as it drove away. They would circle the block.

The light-skinned man was oblivious to our intent as we approached. After one last look around to make sure we didn't have witnesses, I nodded to J-Murder.

"I got him," he smiled.

When we were a few feet from the light-skinned man, J-

Murder pulled the nine and slapped him in the face so hard I thought he knocked out a row of his teeth.

"Ah!" the big man screamed, crumpling to the ground.

"Shut yo' bitch-ass up, nigga! And you bet not move," J-Murder said forcefully as he checked the man for a weapon.

"Okay, son! Okay!"

A few seconds later the van pulled up. Kent and J-Murder threw the light-skinned man inside.

"Yo, what the fuck is this, son? Y'all niggas buggin'. What ch'all on, fam?"

"Is Luther in the building?" Kent asked, pointing a pistol in his face.

I watched questions and answers play out on the light-skinned man's face. And then he told a lie. "I-I don't know Luther. I was just goin' in there to cop sumthin'."

Luke pulled the Mac-12 and pointed it in his face. "What's yo' name, nigga?"

"Spaz. My name Spaz."

"Check this out, Spaz. You got one more time to lie to me, and I'ma let my Mac spaz out on yo' ass. We watched you go in the building. Stop playing and save yo' life. Don't be stupid."

I enjoyed watching Luke be a gangster. My nigga had graduated to being a boss, and Spaz believed him.

"Listen, if you let me go, I'll tell you about the whole operation. I don't got no loyalty to Luther or the Gucci Boyz. I just met them niggas, and I ain't dyin' for none of them niggas, son. Word is bond."

Luke put the pistol away. "We listening."

"The money in apartment seven. That's the safe house. Don't nobody live in the apartment, but it's a camera outside the door so Luther can see everybody that go in and out. Skip and Lockdown out front on security. They been smokin' sherm, so they ain't all the way live. They always slippin'.

Females live in most the apartments downstairs. Niggas got they side pieces or baby mommas up in them joints. Upstairs in six, seven, and eight is where it's at. Luther lay his head in eight."

"What's in apartment six?" I asked.

"That's where niggas kick it at. Meetings an' shit."

"How many people in building?" Waldo asked.

"I don't know about downstairs. When we come in the building, we go right up to six. I seen Luther, Poppy, Manny, and Stills. Like I said, I don't know about downstairs. Am I good? Can I go?"

"Nah, not yet," Luke answered. "You might be setting us up to get knocked off. You coming in the building with us. Matter fact, you taking us in."

"Aw, c'mon, son! If them niggas see me, I'm hit. Just let me get out right here, B. I neva seen none of y'all. Word is bond."

"You don't gotta worry 'bout them niggas doing nothing to you. Luther ain't leaving that building alive," Luke promised.

When Waldo parked in front of The Matrix, Kent and J-Murder hopped out behind Spaz. I watched from the backseat as they exchanged a few words with the niggas on security. After a tension-easing laugh, J-Murder and Kent pulled silenced pistols and killed the shermed-out duo on the front steps.

As soon as the bodies hit the ground, Luke, Waldo, and I followed the trio into the building. There was a short hallway with apartments on both sides. To the immediate right was a flight of stairs. We followed Spaz to apartment six. It was the first door on the right, and it was already open.

J-Murder shoved Spaz into the apartment, sending him crashing through a table. Drinks and ashtrays went flying. While the three men in the living room dropped the Xbox controllers, trying to figure out what was going on, the silenced pistols started clapping along with Luke's loud-ass Mac-12. There were a few screams as The Gucci Boyz were gunned down where they sat.

A short hallway next to the living room got my attention. I moved to check the rooms, letting my silenced nine millimeter lead the way. Waldo followed. There were three doors. I opened the first one. It was an empty bedroom.

Waldo spun toward the second door as it opened. Luther held a 12-gauge pump. He was less than ten feet away, and the shotgun sounded like a dragon's roar as it boomed. Waldo wasn't ready, nor were his reflexes fast enough to react. The slug hit him in the torso, lifting him off the ground and slamming him into the wall.

Luther chambered another round, but I reacted quickly, squeezing the trigger on my pistol until he fell on the ground. Seven bullets hit him in the face, chest, and stomach.

"Baby, you good?" Luke asked, rushing to my side.

"Yeah. I got Luther. We gotta check the last room."

"Damn! Not my boy," Kent mourned behind us.

Me, Luke, and J-Murder approached the final door in the hall. It turned out to be the bathroom, and it was empty. I had just spun around when there was more shooting. Three shots rang out as Kent went to the ground.

"Pussy-nigga shot Kent!" J-Murder screamed, racing toward the living room.

"Did Waldo leave the keys in the van?" Luke asked.

Before I could respond, there was more shooting.

"I don't know."

"C'mon, baby. Help me check his body," Luke said, bending down to search the dead man's pockets.

I didn't want to touch a dead body, but since Luke only had one good arm, I would have to help him search, and it was nasty. The 12-gauge slug tore a huge chunk out of

Waldo's body, exposing his ribs and innards. Not to mention there was blood everywhere. But I had to help get us the fuck out of the building, so I ignored the grossness and found the keys in his front pocket.

"I got 'em. Where is J-Murder?" I asked, heading for the front door.

"That nigga good," Luke said confidently.

I got my confirmation when I got to the stairwell. Spaz was sprawled out on the stairs, bullets holes in the back of his head. J-Murder stood at the front door.

"C'mon, y'all! We gotta get the fuck outta here!"

J-Blunt

Chapter 22

Luke

"Damn, baby. I can't believe both them niggas got killed," I breathed, running my fingers up and down Syn's back. We were lying on the couch, her on top of me, mulling over how to make our next move without the services of Waldo and Kent.

"You think it's a sign?" she asked.

"Hell, nah!" J-Murder cut in. "Them niggas was stupid. Kent took his eyes off the nigga and got clapped up. Ain't no way he was s'posed to leave Spaz. And Waldo was too slow. Nigga shoulda ducked."

"Didn't you check Spaz after you pistol-whipped him?" Syn asked.

"Yeah. He was naked. He must've grabbed one of them dead niggas' shit. Like I said, Kent slipped. Got distracted by Waldo gettin' offed. That was on them niggas."

"Murder right, baby. Them niggas was slipping. Look at it like this: it might've took them niggas dying to save us. We still in New York. Ain't no sense in leaving without making a move on Reign. We came here to get these niggas off our asses. We got one. We still breathing, so the next move is still on."

Syncere stared up at me like I was Jesus giving the sermon on a mountain. "Damn, baby. Hearing you talk like this and the way you taking care of business got me in awe. You used to be so square, and now you calling shots."

I laughed. "Fuck you. I wasn't no square. I was just… reserved."

It was her turn to laugh. "Nah, baby. You know I love you, but you was a square-ass nigga. When you killed Calico nigga in my office, you started panicking and telling me to

181

call the police. 'It was self defense!'" she imitated.

I gave her a hard slap on the ass. "Get off that bullshit, baby. That was my first kill. That shit changed me."

She leaned in for a kiss. "For the better. And I was the same way. The first time I killed somebody, I hyperventilated and almost passed out."

J-Murder watched us with envy. "I want what y'all got."

"What you talking 'bout, nigga?"

"Seem like y'all love is on lock on every level. I just sat here and watched y'all kiss while talking about the first time y'all clapped niggas up. I ain't neva seen no shit like this. Real life Bonnie and Clyde shit. I want me a Bonnie."

I looked at Syncere. She was my baby. My world. My ride-or-die. She would follow me to hell to have a shootout with the devil. "You gotta go through something to get to this level, Murder. You sure you want to go through that?"

"If I can have millions of dollars, a bitch as bad as Syn, and kiss while we talking 'bout killin' niggas, then yeah. I would go through damn near anything to get that."

***

Cinco was one of the hottest clubs in New York. Five stories, a different vibe on every level. A night club, a foam party, a strip club, a sports bar, and a restaurant on the roof that provided dining under the moon. The plan was simple: split up and see if we could find Reign on one of the five stories. We had all seen pictures of him in the local tabloids. In New York he was larger than life, loved by all, hated by few. And we had the task of killing one of New York's finest.

While Syncere took the nightclub and J-Murder took the foam party, I took the strip club and sports bar. I was currently enjoying some of Midnight's eye candy, impressed by the selection of women. They had every flavor – white, black,

Latin, Asian, tall, short, skinny, thick, and all of them super fine. I currently had one of the main attractions grinding on my lap.

"You got bandz in yo' pocket, or you just happy to see me?" Tokyo said, giving me an over-the-shoulder sex face as she rode my lap.

"I got bandz, and I like what in see," I winked.

Tokyo was Chinese and Puerto Rican. And tall. With her heels on, we were the same height, and I was six-foot-three. And she was super thick, her body perfectly proportioned. Big titties, thick thighs, and an ass so big that when she twerked, it made a nigga lose his breath. And she was fine. Cocoa butter complexion, slanted eyes, and lips that looked like she could suck the skin off a nigga's dick. She had me tempted to show her to my girl so we could take her back to the hotel.

"Bandz will make her dance!" she teased before standing and bending over to touch her toes. The red thong got swallowed by her cheeks, and when she made them clap, I had to go in my pocket to tip the dancer. I didn't have a bill smaller than a twenty, but I didn't mind showing my appreciation.

"What would it take for me to get you up out of here and to my hotel room?" I asked when she sat back on my lap.

She turned and gave me another seductive over-the-shoulder look while grinding on my lap. "I'm not one of those girls, baby. I don't do the tricking thing."

"I'm not asking to be your trick. I'm asking to get to know you better. If the sparks fly, we let them."

She spun around to straddle my lap, giving hypnotizing eye contact as she simulated fucking me. "You're not my type. What happened to your arm?"

"I was involved in a bad business deal. But I'm okay. And if you're not into me, why did you choose to keep me company instead of one of these other niggas stalking you?"

"Because you wasn't stalking me," she smiled. "What kind of business do you do?"

"You asking a lot of questions for me not to be your type."

"I'm not interested in you. I'm interested in your work."

"My line of work is dangerous. Gotta stay a step ahead of the competition."

She touched the sling on my arm. "What happened? Did you fall behind the competition a step or two?"

"Nah. Quite the contrary. I'm the alpha. They all chasing to keep up, and sometimes niggas in the rear get desperate. I'm a boss, baby. In word and deed. You chose me because you recognized the presence of a real nigga."

She leaned forward, bending to suck on my ear lobe. "You think you can handle a night with a bad girl?"

I gripped both of her monstrous ass cheeks. They were soft and hard at the same time. Had my dick on ten. "Reach your hand down and tell me if you can handle a night with a bad boy."

She laughed before leaning back to stare at me. "You so fucking cocky, nigga. And I like that shit. I knew it was something different about you."

I went off script, wanting to see how far this could go. "I'm full of surprises, Tokyo. What time do you get off? I got somebody I want you to meet."

A question shown in her slanted eyes. "Don't be on no bullshit, nigga. I ain't really into surprise."

"It's a good one. My wife is here with me. Downstairs. She wanted to party, and I wanted to chill. We're not perverts or freaks out to fuck any and everybody, but I like you, and she likes what I like. I'm telling you this because this don't gotta be a one-night thing. But for anything to happen, my wife has to be involved. She's my Bonnie."

She stopped grinding on my lap, mischief lighting her

eyes. "Show me her picture."

I pulled out my phone and let her see a few pictures of Syn. Tokyo looked impressed.

"She is pretty. You sure she wants competition?"

I laughed. "No offense to you, Tokyo, because you are one of the baddest women I've ever seen, but my wife is a boss. She owns a strip club and modeling agency. Really popular out west. She is hard to intimidate. Take more than a pretty face and phat ass to make her nervous."

Intrigue shown in her sexy eyes. "I get off at three. Leave me your number."

After a few more dances, Tokyo left to entertain the masses, and I went downstairs to find Syn. She was at the bar looking super fine. She had dyed her hair teal green and wore green contacts as a disguise. Dressed in a tight blue dress, she demanded attention. Some young punk was currently giving her the attention, pulled up at the bar, trying to shoot his shot. When she seen me coming, she dismissed the youngin.

"I see you trynna replace me with a younger, weaker version," I joked.

She kissed me on the lips. "You know you're irreplaceable, baby."

"Glad you recognize that. I ran into somebody upstairs that might be able to help us."

She cocked her head to the side. "Who?"

"Tokyo. She get off at three."

Some kind of anger flashed in her eyes. "You thinking with your dick at a time like this?"

"Nah. I'm doing what's necessary to get the job done. I got a good feeling about this one. Trust me. If it don't go the way we want, we find out what she knows and then get rid of her.

Something like lust and murder shown in her eyes. "Let's see how good your taste in toys is."

***

When we got back to the telly, the drinks flowed and Tokyo lit a stick of loud. I hadn't smoked in a while, so the THC and Aces had me lit. We all sat on the couch, Syncere in the middle, and I watched them interact, anticipating the showdown between my boss bitch and the sexy vixen.

"There are a lot of pretty girls out there, but I haven't seen anything like you. What are your measurements?" Syn asked, pouring another glass of champagne.

"I'm five-ten, 230 pounds, J cups, twenty-five-inch waist, fifty-two-inch hips and ass. And I'm twenty-four."

I didn't know much about a woman's measurements, but I knew those numbers sounded ridiculous. She was truly a rare gem.

"I can do some things for you once I go home. We live in LA. I have a modeling studio, and I own a strip club. Have you done any real print work?"

"Not really. Instagram stuff. Online magazines. Nothing major."

"Well, if you could ever fly out to Los Angeles, I have a few contacts that could help up your exposure. Right now I'm working with Victoria's Secret, trying to get my girls out of the booty magazine world and into high fashion."

Her eyes lit up. "Oh, wow! That would be amazing. I was using this dancing as a hustle while I went through college. I want to open my own business. But if I could do real modeling…."

Syncere had impressed me. Tokyo was clay in my girl's hands, being molded into opportunity.

"I'll help you out if I can. I'll leave you my card. Take some time and come up with a date for you to come to LA. I'll get you the opportunities, but you have to provide your own way. And by the look of you, I know you'll be fine."

Tokyo reached out to hug my girl. "Thank you so much, Syncere. I appreciate this so much. If there is anything I can do for you to show my gratitude, let me know."

"Actually, there is," I cut in. "Tell me about your boss."

"Who, Steve? That's who hired me. Nigga is really a pervert that got some favor with Mr. Reign. Why do you want to know about him?"

"Not Steve. Mr. Reign."

Surprise shown in her eyes. "Oh. He's cool, I guess. I see him around and we talked a little bit, but I'm not his type. He likes the Asian girls."

"If I wanted to set up a meeting, how would I do that?"

"I don't know. Call his assistant, maybe."

"What if I wanted the meeting to be personal? I don't want anybody to know we're having this meeting. It needs to be a surprise."

Confusion shown on her face before she looked to Syncere. "I don't understand what he is talking about."

"We need to get to Mr. Reign. He put my husband in that sling."

A light clicked on in her mind. "Oh." When she realized our intention, her eyes grew wide. "Oh, no! I don't want nothing to do with that. I don't know anything. And I don't got no loyalties to Mr. Reign, but I don't want to be involved. I'm not looking for drama."

"Relax. We don't want you to get involved. This has nothing to do with you. Our business with Mr. Reign is personal. You will not be put in the middle. I just want to know if he has a soft spot. How often is he in the club?"

She looked unsure. "Mr. Reign is a businessman. He hangs with politicians and does stuff for the community. He just opened a community center. How is he the one that put you in a sling. He's a good guy."

"There is lot you don't know about your boss. But one thing is for sure: he ain't a good guy. Tell me how often he is in *Cinco*."

"Um, he's there almost every night. Sushi and Tushi are his girlfriends. They're the Asian girls."

"Did he pick them up tonight?" Syn asked.

"Yeah. He was there while y'all was there. In the back. He spends most of his time in the back room at Midnight. He's normally the last person to leave. But he has bodyguards. Four of them."

I had everything I needed to plot my next move. Syn felt the same way. "Okay, baby. That's all we were asking for. We don't want to involve you. And if you don't feel safe here anymore, you can fly back to LA with us and I will hire you in my club. Whatever you want to do. It's up to you."

"Uh, I'm not sure what I want to do right now. Can I have some time to think about it?"

"You can take as much time as you need. The offer will always be on the table. Is that good with you?"

"Yeah. I'm good."

Syn smiled. "Good. 'Cause I been waiting to see them big-ass titties since we met. Take that dress off, baby."

With a sexy smile, Tokyo stood and gave us what we wanted. Even though I had already seen her in a thong and bra, seeing her butt-naked was something else. Her skin tone was flawless. Not a wrinkle or smudge. And that ass. Oh my God!

"Baby, you better dick her ass down!" Syn smiled lustfully, grabbing two handfuls of one of Tokyo's monster ass cheeks.

"I plan on it," I said, sitting up and removing my sports jacket.

When Syn stood and undressed, the ladies got touchy-feely. And even though the twenty-four-year-old stripper was stacked and on top of her shit, so was my boss bitch. At forty years old, my baby was put together like she could entertain niggas on a stage. Nice titties, slim waist, and a phat ass I loved drilling from the back.

The women stood before me, kissing, rubbing titties, and grabbing ass. When they fell onto the couch, Syn was on top, letting her fingers go to work on Tokyo's bald pussy while her lips sucked them big ass titties. My dick felt like it was going to bust out of my pants as I watched Tokyo moan and make the kind of sex faces that could get her an adult film award.

When she was good and wet, Syn tagged me in. "Get undressed, baby. I got her hot for you."

I stood and tried to undress as fast as I could. With one arm it was a tall task, so they helped. When I was naked, they got on their knees before me and worshipped my dick. They took turns giving me head and playing with my balls.

After having some fun with their tongues, I was ready for some pussy. Specifically, Tokyo's. Her lips were fat, and I couldn't wait to have them wrapped around my dick. When I sat on the couch, she eased down onto my pole, reverse cowgirl. Her pussy was snug and wet as fuck. After getting her rhythm, she began bouncing that ass. And she was a rider, too. She knew how to get hers. I used my good arm to hold one of her hips as she rode me. Syn's lips joined the party, kneeling in front of Tokyo and sucking her clit as she rode me.

The sex kitten was no match for my dick and Syncere's lips. When she climaxed, baby girl came like a water fountain.

J-Blunt

Chapter 23

Syn

We spent the next three days watching *Cinco*'s operations and the movements of Reign. During the daylight hours, he was surrounded by people – three or four bodyguards, an assistant or two, and a few women, normally Sushi and Tushi. They went all over New York, presumably taking care of business. Night time was a different story. He often came to the club with two bodyguards and conducted business in the back office of Midnight.

Luke, J-Murder, and I watched him in plain sight at the club, monitoring the comings and goings of Mr. Reign and his people. He normally left the club at 3:00 AM, with Sushi, Tushi, and two bodyguards in a black SUV. The plan we came up with was brazen. Hit the truck and kill everyone inside, especial Reign.

We were waiting in the alley behind *Cinco*, hiding amongst the garbage cans and the back doors of nearby businesses. When I heard the truck's automatic start turn over the engine, my armpits began to sweat. It was almost time. I clutched the butt of the silenced pistol, ready to end all of my problems of the last two years. Luke crouched beside me, holding the other silenced pistol. J-Murder was on the other side of the alley with the Mac-12, waiting for the driver. I had the passenger. Luke would kill everybody in the backseat. Easy as pie.

When the back door opened, two bodyguards stepped out to look around. After they were satisfied the coast was clear, one opened the SUV's back door. Sushi and Tushi were the first ones to get in the truck, followed by Mr. Reign. When the precious cargo was tucked away, one bodyguard hopped in the passenger seat while the other walked around to the driver's side of the truck.

J-Murder's timing was perfect. As soon as the guard reached for the door, the Mac-12 started talking, dropping him before he knew what hit him. Luke and I leapt from our hiding spots, the silenced pistols clapping. I aimed for the passenger. Luke had the back seat.

Sparks flew as our bullets hit the windows and side paneling. And to my surprise and horror, not one piece of our lead penetrated the windows or truck's frame. Our bullets bounced off the bulletproofing, not even leaving a scratch or dent.

Reign spun to look out the window, a smile on his face after we made eye contact.

"Shit! It's bulletproof!" I screamed, realizing we were in no man's land.

Luke grabbed a door handle, trying to yank the door open. It was locked. There was no way we would be able to get to Reign. We had no choice but to run.

Luke read my mind. "Run, baby! Run!"

The stupid thing about the alley behind *Cinco* was there was only one way in and one way out. The buildings were so close together that we couldn't run between them. On top of that, the club was in the middle of a long-ass block. We had to run at least a hundred yards to get to safety. Good thing I had on running shoes. I hauled ass like I was in a hundred-meter relay. Luke ran alongside me, J-Murder close behind, bringing up the rear.

We were almost to the end of the alley when they started shooting at us. "Aw, shit!" J-Murder screamed

I turned my head as he fell to the ground.

Luke stopped, crouching in a doorway and shooting back. "Keep going! Get to the car! J-Murder, get up, nigga!"

I didn't argue. He was buying me time. I took advantage of it. The car was a few feet from the mouth of the alley, keys in the ignition. I jumped in the driver's seat and started the car when Luke came flying around the corner.

"Go, baby, go!" he screamed after diving in the passenger seat.

I paused. "What about J-Murder?"

He tried to be strong, but I could see the pain on his face. "He gone, baby. Go!"

***

We lost another one.

Every time I closed my eyes, the words popped into my mind like they were written on the back of my eyelids. Everybody who had gotten close to us ended up in a body bag. Why Luke and I were still alive, I didn't know, but I was thankful to be in bed, lying next to my nigga, tucked safely away at our house in Fox Lake.

"Everybody around us keeps dying, Luke. What the fuck is going on?" I vented, wiping tears from my eyes. I had been crying for days. Every time I remembered J-Murder, Tahiti, Trinity, or Jayda, the tears rolled. I was responsible for all their deaths, and the guilt was eating me alive.

"I wish I knew, baby," he breathed. "I wish I knew."

"I don't want nobody else to die. I'm tired of losing people. I can't stop thinking about Trinity, J-Murder, and Tahiti. They were kids, baby. This shit is tearing at my soul. I can't ignore the pain no more."

"I feel it too, baby. And I don't know what to do about it. I think we just have to give it some time. Focus on trying to make the best out of our futures."

We grew quiet for a few moments before Luke spoke again. "Damn, baby. We had that nigga. We could've ended all this shit. If Reign would've died, maybe it wouldn't feel like everybody died for nothing. Nigga had a bulletproof truck. What are the chances of that shit?"

"I thought that shit was for the President. We have to figure out another move, because he's coming for us again. I looked him in the eyes. He knew it was me."

"We're running out of options, baby. We probably won't be able to get close to him again, at least not for a while. We might've lost our only opportunity to get that nigga."

"Do you want to leave? Try to get away for a while and lay low?"

"As much as I hate to say it, leaving might be our only chance at survival. He's coming for us again. I know it. We need to get out of the country for a couple months. Plus, I need some time for my arm to heal."

"Okay. I'm in. I'll book our flights tomorrow. I need a break from all this. Where do you want to go?"

"What you think about Puerto Rico? We don't need passports, and we can blend in easily. Plus, the cost of living is cheap."

"Sounds good to me. I don't care where we go as long as I'm with you."

After a round of sex and getting off twice, we curled up and fell asleep. I was awakened a couple hours later by the need to pee. I grabbed my phone to check the time. It was 3:33 AM.

I had just climbed out of bed when a strange feeling overcame me. Something was wrong. My intuition never lied. I looked down at Luke and seen him sleeping peacefully. I wanted to wake him, but didn't. Instead, I went to pee. I was walking through the living room when something caught my eye. One of the curtains was slightly open. A dark-colored SUV was parked out front, and people dressed in black were climbing out. For a moment my feet were glued to the ground. I knew it was Reign. But how did he find us? Shit!

When my feet got unstuck, I ran to the room and snatched

the nine-millimeter Ruger with the fifty-round drum from the bedside table. "Luke, get up! I think Reign is outside!"

He leapt out of the bed like a soldier trained for war and snatched the pistol from my hand. "Gimme that. You get the AR. Where the nigga at?"

"They out front. I seen at least four if them," I said as I climbed under the bed to get the AR-15.

When we were strapped, I followed Luke down the hallway, stopping at the threshold to the living room and kitchen. Luke pointed the pistol at the back door. I pointed the assault rifle at the front door, holding my breath, listening, expecting it to pop off at any moment.

It was eerily quiet. And then I heard the knob on the front door twist. It was locked. I wanted to start shooting, but I remembered what happened when I tried to shoot Vega through the door. I wasn't going to make that mistake again. All fifty bullets in this clip would count.

And I didn't have to wait long. There was a loud crash as the front door flew open. Two people in black rushed in. I pulled the trigger as fast as I could. The first one caught it the worst, bullets hitting him in the face and torso, falling him onto his partner. I tore the second one up, too, hitting him up until he crumbled to the floor.

When the back door exploded off the hinges, Luke let the pistol ride, dropping the intruder. I was about to turn the AR his way to help, but I had more action at the front door. Two more people had run in the house, and they carried those damn space guns.

I hit the first one high in the chest and neck, and he went down. The second one made it into the house, and I couldn't get a lock on him before he started shooting. The space gun sounded like God was screaming at us as pieces of the wall exploded behind my head. We did the only thing we could do and retreated to the bedroom. Luke closed the door behind us as we dove on the floor, staying low.

The space guns erupted again, blowing the door apart.

"It's too many of them, baby!" I cried, finally realizing the end of us might be near. Those guns scared the shit out of me. Had me scared to move.

Luke didn't share my fear. He was lying on the floor, hiding behind the wall, firing blindly down the hall. The goons fired back with their big guns, but didn't make a move to come in the room.

Then everything went quiet. For a moment I thought they left the house, until I heard something bouncing on the floor. Two round metal balls slid into the room. I didn't know what they were. But Luke did.

"Shit! Syncere!"

Boom! Boom!

The blasts blew out the windows, emitting a bright white flash that blinded me. I couldn't see shit, and my ears were ringing like an alarm was going off in my head.

Strong hands grabbed me, forcing me onto my stomach, tying my hands behind my back and putting a hood over my head. They drug me out of the house and shoved me into the truck.

The drive was quiet. After about an hour, the truck stopped and I was manhandled again, led into what smelled like a barn. I could hear horses neighing and feel hay under my feet.

After being thrown to my knees, another body was sat next to me. I knew it was Luke.

"Take the hoods off," someone commanded.

When the hood was snatched off my head, I looked around the barn for a moment before my eyes landed on a light-skinned man in a tailored black suit. He was tall, six-four or six-five with broad shoulders, a muscular build, and looked just like Calico. Four men dressed in black and carrying space guns stood next to him.

"You muthafuckas was a pain in the ass, I'll tell you that. I'ma make this simple. Which one of y'all killed my little brother? Where is the body?"

"I killed him. He tried to extort me," I said, hoping my confession would spare Luke's life.

"No, she didn't," Luke spoke up. "I did it. I shot him."

Reign sucked his teeth, looking us over. "Okay. I see how this is going to go. This that ride-or-die shit. I get it. So, I'ma give one of y'all the opportunity to live. Start from the beginning Loretta. Be brief, because I got shit to do."

"I killed him, nigga. I told you it was me," Luke said.

Mr. Reign kicked him in the face, sending him sprawling to the floor. "If you speak again without being addressed, I'ma kill both of y'all. Pick him back up and put him on his knees. Tell me the story, Loretta."

I glanced at Luke, pleading with my eyes for him to let me handle this. "Twenty years ago I killed the nigga that tried to rape me and took his money. Turned out he worked for Calico and had his money. One hundred thousand dollars. When I got out of prison, I opened a strip club and Calico tried to extort me. He tried to kill me and kidnapped my daughter, so I killed him."

Reign stared at me for a long time, like he was looking through my soul. Then he nodded. "Damn. This shit is so stupid. You mean to tell me he died over one hundred lousy-ass thousand dollars? Stupid-ass nigga. Okay. Where is the body?"

"I don't know. Luke got rid of him."

He turned to Luke. "She telling the truth?"

He spun to look at me, love, regret, and misery written all over his swelling face. "Yeah. She telling the truth."

"Alright. Where is the body? I need to send him to our parents."

"I cremated him in a burn pit and threw the ashes in a creek. He gone."

Reign looked irritated. Then he checked his watch. "Okay. I got shit to do. One of y'all get to live. You decide," he said, pulling a chrome pistol from his waist. After taking out the clip, he sat the gun on the floor in front of us. "One shot. Imani, cut their wrists loose."

One of the men with space guns used a knife to cut the ties from our wrists, then they pointed the space guns at us. This was it, how our story would end. There was no way out. One of us had to go.

"Go ahead, baby," Luke cried, tears spilling down his face. "Do it. Shoot me. Live."

I cried with him. "No. I can't. I'm the reason all of this happened. All this is my fault. I can't go on without you. You all I have left. If you're not with me, I don't have a reason to live. I lost everybody I loved. You have your parents and Latia. And Barron. They need you. Shoot me."

Luke was stubborn. "No. I'm not touching that gun. Get it over with. Do it."

"Somebody better do something before I take my order back," Reign said impatiently.

There was no sense in both of us dying. Somebody had to make a choice. So I did. I reached for the pistol, crying harder than I had ever cried in my whole life. I didn't want our story to be over with. I wanted more time. There was so much we didn't get the chance to do. He hadn't even turned thirty. We were too young to die. But there was no way out of this one. This was it. The end of our story.

"I'm sorry, Luke. I will always love you." I closed my eyes, lifting the gun to my head and squeezing the trigger.

"No!" Luke screamed.

The gun clicked, but there was no boom.

I looked up at Reign. He took the pistol, wearing an

amused smile. "You didn't think I was actually going to give you a loaded gun, did you?" he asked before popping the clip in the gun and chambering a round. "I made my choice. Let this be a lesson, Luke. Fuck love."

Boom!

The worst pain I ever felt in my life coursed through my body. It felt like I had been stabbed in the heart, and then my heart was snatched from my body and thrown into a fiery volcano. That's how it felt watching Luke get shot in the head. His body fell backward, the strength gone from his limbs as he fell.

"No! Luke! No!" I screamed, crawling on top of him. There was a hole in his forehead, and when I lifted his head off the straw, I felt blood and brains oozing out of the hole in the back of his head.

It took a couple of seconds for the life to drain from his eyes.

"Hold that bitch down," Reign ordered.

His henchmen grabbed me off Luke and slammed me to the ground, pinning my limbs to the floor. I tried to resist, but Reign knelt on top of my chest, making it hard for me to breathe. He looked into my eyes, grabbing me by the hair. "You took someone I loved from me, so I took someone you loved from you. He had every reason to live. You didn't. Now you have to live with his death on your hands for the rest of your life. And I just need one more thing before I go."

I struggled to no avail as he took a knife from one of his men. Then he dug it into my right eye. The second worst pain I ever felt was him taking my eye.

"An eye for an eye, Loretta. Let this be your lesson. Don't fuck with Mr. Reign."

J-Blunt

Epilogue

Three Months Later

When I awoke, before I opened my eyes, the first thing I did was reach across the bed for Luke. But he was gone. My eyes shot open, searching the room for my man. His phone was sitting on the bedside table, and his clothes were still on the floor, so I knew he hadn't gone far. After a yawn and stretch, I grabbed my phone to check the time. 9:35 AM. Time for me to shower and get dressed for work. I had an important meeting with a stranger looking to invest in my strip club.

After climbing out of bed, I went to the bathroom to freshen up. I had just turned on the shower when Luke showed up at the door.

"Good morning, baby," he smiled.

I looked over my shoulder at the love of my life. He was tall, fine, and amazing – everything I ever wanted in a man. "Hey, baby. I was looking for you when I woke up."

"I was downstairs. What are you up to?"

"I have a meeting. Somebody wants to invest in the club. I really don't want any investors, but I have to listen, right?"

"Yeah, you do. Want me to get in there with you?" he asked, nodding toward the shower.

"No," I laughed. "Messing with you, I'll be late for my meeting. Get out."

He gave me a sexy smile before leaving. "Your loss."

After a shower, I brushed my teeth and went to get dressed. I settled on a purple pantsuit. I had to look bossy for the meeting. After I was satisfied with my look, I popped in my glass eye before grabbing my phone to check my messages. I had a bunch from Vanessa, my psychiatrist. I decided I would call her on the drive to The Den of Syn.

"Luke, I'm leaving, baby. I'll call you later," I called

before leaving the house.

After some debate, I grudgingly called Vanessa.

"Hi, Syncere. I was wondering if you would ever return my calls."

"To be honest, Vanessa, I really didn't want to call you back."

"I can tell. I haven't seen you in a couple weeks. Seems like you're avoiding me. I just wanted to know how you are doing."

"I'm doing well. On my way to work to meet a potential investor. I'm good."

"That's great. So, I take it you've adjusted to being back at work?"

"Yeah. Everyone is giving me space and respecting my boundaries. It's only been a week, but I feel like things are finally getting back to normal."

There was a pause on her end of her line. "What about Luke? Is he still showing up?"

It was my turn to pause. Luke was dead, had been for three months, but my house was still filled with his things, and my heart was still filled with love for my man. And for the last few weeks, everyday and at all times throughout the day, he showed up to keep me company. I knew it was all in my head and I might be going crazy, but I allowed the scenes with Luke to play out because having him around made me feel sane. The first time he showed up I was scared as hell, but talking with him was what made me get back to living life.

"Yeah. I just seen him before I left the house."

"What did he say?"

I thought about lying. I didn't like talking to her about Luke. "He wanted to get in the shower with me," I laughed.

She laughed, too. "Oh. Okay. Well, things sound like they are good. How about you make an appointment soon so we can talk more about Luke showing up. Maybe there is a way to control his comings and goings to help you cope with his loss better."

This was why I didn't want to tell her about him. I didn't want him to leave. "Listen, Vanessa. I know this is not normal. I know Luke is dead, and I know it's not really him showing up. But this has helped me get back to living. Before he showed up, I was locked in my house for two months, only talking to people through text messages. I don't went to get rid of him. Losing him was the worst pain I'd ever felt in my life. Even worse than losing my eye. I didn't want to eat, drink, take a shower, or even talk to another person. I don't want to go through that again. I know he's not really here, but I loved him so much that I'll take whatever time I can have with him, even if it's all in my head. He completes me. I'm good as long as he's here."

"Okay. I don't want to push you. I just want to help. Schedule a meeting so we can talk about this some more."

I had already made up my mind. I was done with Vanessa. All I needed was my man. "Okay. I'll check my calendar and get back to you."

When I got to the club, Diamond greeted me with a smile as soon as I walked in the door. "Hi, Syncere. Mr. Lee is here," she said, pointing toward the main stage.

I was surprised my guest was already waiting for me. The meeting wasn't for another thirty minutes. He was a small Japanese man that was probably older than me, but I couldn't tell his age. Asians and black people aged really good. He wore a dark tailored suit, and I guessed him to be important since he was surrounded by three bodyguards.

"Mr. Lee?" I asked, extending my hand. "I'm Syncere. You're kind of early."

He stood and shook my hand. "Ah, you are very beautiful, and it is a pleasure to finally meet the owner of this wonderful club," he said in perfect English. "I showed up early to enjoy some of the entertainment before we meet. I really like the talent you've acquired."

"Thank you for the compliments. Would you like to go to my office and talk?"

"Yes. Please."

I led him to my office, his bodyguards following and standing outside the door. "Have a seat. Would you like somethin' to drink?"

"Yes. Whatever you have, I'll have," he smiled.

I poured glasses of vodka before sitting behind my desk. "So, I understand you have a business proposal. As you know, I'm not looking for investors. But since you insisted on this meeting, I'll listen."

"Thank you. I know you don't want investors, but I believe I may have an offer you cannot refuse. First, I would like to show you my vision," he said before pulling out his phone. After finding what he was looking for, he handed me the phone. On the screen was a building that looked like a sports arena with futuristic designs.

"What is it?" I asked.

"It is called The Phoenix. A new way to entertain the masses. A seven-story, one-stop place for all kinds of entertainment. A dance club, gentlemen's club, restaurants, shopping stores, a spa, a game hall with the latest video games. This will be the new way to entertain. I have a friend with a five-story building that inspired the idea. I want to take it to another sphere. In America, bigger is better."

I slid the phone across the desk. "Well, I'm flattered you want to talk to me about this, but I don't see how I can help you. You need more land."

He smiled. "Precisely. I want to buy your land. And I will offer you twice what it is worth."

I chuckled. "I'm sorry, but I'm not looking to sell. I'm fine with my business."

"Please reconsider, my dear. I would like to make a multi-million-dollar investment on this land, and you are the key. Name your price."

I sat back in my chair to study the small man. The only way someone would over pay for a business was if they could make more. Investing millions into this land wouldn't be worth shit. Unless he knew something I didn't.

"Why is this land so important? What do you know."

The smile that crossed his face told me I was onto something. "You are an intriguing woman. Your intuition is sharp. What happened to your eye?"

I blinked a few times, trying to think of an answer. I wasn't expecting the question. "This was the price of a valuable lesson. Let's get back to the task at hand. What do you know?"

"There are plans for this area. I want to be first in line."

I waited for him to say more, but he didn't. And that was okay. I had everything I needed. "I'm sorry, Mr. Lee, but I'm not looking to sell."

His eyes dimmed. "That is very unfortunate, ma'am. I would've made you a very rich woman. But here is my card if you change your mind. Thank you for your time."

***

"How was work?" Luke asked when I walked into the bedroom.

"It was okay. I spent most of the day at the modeling agency. Do you remember Tokyo?"

He grinned. "Shit, how could I forget. Her ass was ginormous," he laughed.

"She called me today. Wants to come to LA to join the team. She will be a great addition to the agency. She can be the new Ashley Grahm."

"That sounds good, baby. What about that meeting with the investor? How did that go?"

"A little Asian man wants to buy the land and turn it into a seven-story mega-complex. Shopping, strip club, restaurants, a dance club. Said he has a friend that – Oh my God!"

"What, baby? Are you okay?" Luke asked.

I stared at him for a long time without speaking, my eyes wide with surprise. It couldn't be. It had to be some kind of coincidence.

"What, baby?"

Hearing Luke's voice snapped me out of my trance. I grabbed my purse and emptied it onto the bed. When I found the card, I dialed the number.

"Syncere, how are you?" Mr. Lee answered. "Have you called to renegotiate?"

"Yes. Uh, I gave it some thought, and I would like to discuss it a little more."

"Unfortunately, I am not in LA anymore, and I won't be in the country for a few weeks."

"Okay. Um, I have a few business trips lined up as well. Is there any chance you'll be in New York anytime soon?"

"As a matter of fact, I am. I'll be in New York in two weeks."

"So will I. I have a conference. Would you like to meet then?"

"That is fine with me. I have the perfect spot for us to meet. Have you ever heard of *Cinco*?"

***

The New York suburb was quiet. The working class people of the neighborhood had self-given curfews. On a Sunday night at almost midnight, everyone was sleep, preparing for a longest day of the week: Monday.

Near the end of the block was a blue-and-green house. All the lights were off except the one in the bedroom. Marshall Jackson sat in a chair at the bedside, watching the show unfold on the king sized mattress. Two Asian women in thongs and bras put on a sexy show, freaking each other and getting him hot and bothered. They kissed, groped, rubbed, and grinded.

Marshall was caught up in the show, oblivious to the masked men standing on the front porch. A loud crash at the front door echoed through the house. The federal agent went for the service pistol on the nightstand.

Tushi was faster, grabbing the gun before the fed could arm himself.

"What the fuck are you doing?" he barked, fear in his eyes as he reached for the gun. "Gimme that!"

Instead of giving him the gun, she threw it on the floor. Before he could pick it up, four armed men ran in the room.

"Touch that gun and I'ma blow your brains out!" one of the gunmen yelled. "Get your hands up."

Agent Jackson lifted his hands in the air. "I am a federal agent. You are making a big mistake. Leave my house right now and I'll give you a head start."

The gunman in charge smiled at the wise words, but instead of responding, he lowered the gun and pulled out a Taser. The projectiles hit agent Jackson in the chest, dropping him on the bed, his body spasming as thousands of volts of electricity flowed through his body.

"You talk too fucking much," Virgil hissed before pressing the key on his com. "Strong Man to Eagle."

"This is Eagle," a smooth voice said over the radio.

"The package is secure. We're en route to the rendezvous. ETA, ten minutes."

"Eagle copies. I can't wait."

The rendezvous point was an abandoned warehouse. When the black SUV pulled into the building, Mr. Reign's smile grew wider, anticipating the moment.

After parking, Virgil pulled the handcuffed federal agent from the back seat and threw him to the ground.

"Well, well, well. Turns out yo' bitch-ass ain't invincible after all," Mr. Reign laughed.

"Fuck you, coward. Tell your boys to let me go and I'll show you how *invincible* I am."

Reign laughed, pulling a pistol from his waist. "The fake display of bravado is cute, but this meeting will be short-lived. I wanted to be the last face you seen before you meet the maker. Goodbye, Agent Jackson."

Seven shots to the body dropped the fed onto his back. And just to make sure he was dead, Mr. Reign stood over him and emptied the clip in his face.

"Damn, that felt good!" he breathed. "Clean this up, fellas. Virgil, you're with me. I have a meeting to attend. Let's go."

***

Back at Midnight, Mr. Reign poured drinks into crystal glasses for him and his guest before settling behind the big oak desk.

"You seem to be in an exceptional mood," Mr. Lee smiled, noticing the spring in his partner's step.

"You ever heard of a rapper named Tupac Shakur?"

The Asian man paused to think for a moment. "I can't say that I have. Not a fan of aggressive lyrics."

"Tupac was different than most of the garbage you hear today. He was a poet. One of my favorite lines was from his song called *Hail Mary*. 'Revenge is like the sweetest joy, next to getting pussy.'"

Mr. Lee thought on the quote. "How true," he said before the men shared a laugh. "I also have a bit of good news to share. I'm about to enter the nightclub business of sorts. Thanks to your brainchild, *Cinco*, I've come up with my own mega-complex. The Phoenix."

Reign laughed. "Oh, yeah? Give me the logistics."

"It'll be out west. In LA. The governor told me they will be building a new stadium in two years near the property site. Talking millions of dollars in revenue every quarter. The Phoenix will be seven stories. Everything you want will be provided. And my business partner already has quite the following at her strip club. All the stars are in regular attendance."

"What's the name of this club that all the stars attend? I might know it."

"It's called the Den of Syn. It'll be on the seventh floor of my complex."

Mr. Reign's smile became sinister. "I've heard of the place. And I know the owner. I took a souvenir from her recently."

Mr. Lee looked puzzled. "You've met, Syncere? She said she didn't know you."

"You discussed me with her?"

"Yes. I told her you were the inspiration for my idea. I brought her to *Cinco* to show her the layout."

Mr. Reign's disposition changed from entertained to enraged. "You brought her to my club? Where is she now?"

"She's out on the floor. I told her I would introduce her to you. Is everything okay?"

Reign walked over to the security monitor and searched the cameras until he found her. "Virgil, go get that bitch and bring her to my office!"

The bodyguard snapped into action, taking another guard with him as they hurried from the office.

"Mr. Reign, what is going on? How do you know Syncere?"

He took a moment to get his breathing under control. "I took her eye."

When the office door opened, Syncere was escorted in by Virgil. She smiled, appearing happy. She was wearing a pantsuit, the top appearing puffy like she was hiding something or gained weight.

"What the fuck are you doing in my club?" Reign barked.

"I had to come see you. When Mr. Lee said he would introduce me, I dropped everything and came over."

Reign looked puzzled. Then he got mad. "You got about ten seconds to tell me what the fuck you talking about before I take more then your other eye."

When Syncere opened her purse, Virgil reached for his pistol.

"It's just a phone," she said, pulling it out, holding it toward Mr. Reign. "It's a call. Luke wants to talk to you."

Mr. Reign stared at her for moment. And that's when he realized she had gone crazy. The smile on her face and sadistic look in her eyes told him she had lost her mind.

"Luke is dead. Virgil, kill this bitch."

The bodyguard lifted the gun toward her head, preparing to execute her. Syncere smiled, continuing to hold the phone and take steps toward Mr. Reign. Before Virgil could squeeze the trigger, Syncere pushed a button on the phone.

It rang, detonating the bomb wrapped around her body. The explosion rocked the office, blowing out the walls and windows, killing most of those present instantly.

Mr. Reign lay on his back, staring wide-eyed at the crumbling ceiling, feeling the heat from the fire and water from the sprinkler system. Everything around him was blackened, burned, and on fire. The excruciating pain shooting through his body told of the damage.

And then blackness came creeping in.

The End

Submission Guideline

Submit the first three chapters of your completed manuscript to ldpsubmissions@gmail.com, subject line: Your book's title. The manuscript must be in a .doc file and sent as an attachment. Document should be in Times New Roman, double spaced and in size 12 font. Also, provide your synopsis and full contact information. If sending multiple submissions, they must each be in a separate email.

Have a story but no way to send it electronically? You can still submit to LDP/Ca$h Presents. Send in the first three chapters, written or typed, of your completed manuscript to:

LDP: Submissions Dept
Po Box 870494
Mesquite, Tx 75187

DO NOT send original manuscript. Must be a duplicate.

Provide your synopsis and a cover letter containing your full contact information.

Thanks for considering LDP and Ca$h Presents.

<u>Coming Soon from Lock Down Publications/Ca$h Presents</u>

BOW DOWN TO MY GANGSTA

By **Ca$h**

TORN BETWEEN TWO

By **Coffee**

BLOOD STAINS OF A SHOTTA **III**

By **Jamaica**

STEADY MOBBIN **III**

By **Marcellus Allen**

RENEGADE BOYS IV

By Meesha

BLOOD OF A BOSS **VI**

SHADOWS OF THE GAME II

By **Askari**

LOYAL TO THE GAME **IV**

By **T.J. & Jelissa**

A DOPEBOY'S PRAYER **II**

By **Eddie "Wolf" Lee**

IF LOVING YOU IS WRONG… **III**

By **Jelissa**

TRUE SAVAGE **VII**

By **Chris Green**

BLAST FOR ME **III**

DUFFLE BAG CARTEL **IV**

HEARTLESS GOON **II**

By **Ghost**

J-Blunt

A HUSTLER'S DECEIT III

KILL ZONE **II**

BAE BELONGS TO ME III

SOUL OF A MONSTER III

By **Aryanna**

THE COST OF LOYALTY **III**

By **Kweli**

THE SAVAGE LIFE II

By **J-Blunt**

KING OF NEW YORK V

RISE TO POWER III

COKE KINGS IV

BORN HEARTLESS II

By **T.J. Edwards**

GORILLAZ IN THE BAY IV

De'Kari

THE STREETS ARE CALLING II

Duquie Wilson

KINGPIN KILLAZ IV

STREET KINGS III

PAID IN BLOOD III

CARTEL KILLAZ II

Hood Rich

SINS OF A HUSTLA II

ASAD

TRIGGADALE III

Elijah R. Freeman

KINGZ OF THE GAME IV

Playa Ray

SLAUGHTER GANG IV

RUTHLESS HEART II

By Willie Slaughter

THE HEART OF A SAVAGE II

By Jibril Williams

FUK SHYT II

By Blakk Diamond

THE DOPEMAN'S BODYGAURD II

By Tranay Adams

TRAP GOD II

By Troublesome

YAYO II

By S. Allen

GHOST MOB

Stilloan Robinson

KINGPIN DREAMS

By Paper Boi Rari

CREAM

By Yolanda Moore

SON OF A DOPE FIEND II

By Renta

<u>Available Now</u>

<u>RESTRAINING ORDER **I & II**</u>

J-Blunt

By **CA$H & Coffee**

LOVE KNOWS NO BOUNDARIES **I II & III**

By **Coffee**

RAISED AS A GOON I, II, III & IV

BRED BY THE SLUMS I, II, III

BLAST FOR ME I & II

ROTTEN TO THE CORE I II III

A BRONX TALE I, II, III

DUFFEL BAG CARTEL I II III

HEARTLESS GOON

A SAVAGE DOPEBOY

HEARTLESS GOON

By **Ghost**

LAY IT DOWN **I & II**

LAST OF A DYING BREED

BLOOD STAINS OF A SHOTTA I & II

By **Jamaica**

LOYAL TO THE GAME

LOYAL TO THE GAME II

LOYAL TO THE GAME III

LIFE OF SIN I, II III

By **TJ & Jelissa**

BLOODY COMMAS I & II

SKI MASK CARTEL I II & III

KING OF NEW YORK I II,III IV

RISE TO POWER I II

COKE KINGS I II III

BORN HEARTLESS

216

A Gangster's Syn 3

By **T.J. Edwards**

IF LOVING HIM IS WRONG…I & II

LOVE ME EVEN WHEN IT HURTS I II III

By **Jelissa**

WHEN THE STREETS CLAP BACK I & II III

By **Jibril Williams**

A DISTINGUISHED THUG STOLE MY HEART I II & III

LOVE SHOULDN'T HURT I II III IV

RENEGADE BOYS I II III

By **Meesha**

A GANGSTER'S CODE I &, II III

A GANGSTER'S SYN I II III

THE SAVAGE LIFE

By J-Blunt

PUSH IT TO THE LIMIT

By **Bre' Hayes**

BLOOD OF A BOSS **I, II, III, IV, V**

SHADOWS OF THE GAME

By **Askari**

THE STREETS BLEED MURDER **I, II & III**

THE HEART OF A GANGSTA I II& III

By **Jerry Jackson**

CUM FOR ME

CUM FOR ME 2

CUM FOR ME 3

CUM FOR ME 4

CUM FOR ME 5

An **LDP Erotica Collaboration**

BRIDE OF A HUSTLA **I II & II**

THE FETTI GIRLS **I, II& III**

CORRUPTED BY A GANGSTA I, II III, IV

BLINDED BY HIS LOVE

By **Destiny Skai**

WHEN A GOOD GIRL GOES BAD

By **Adrienne**

THE COST OF LOYALTY I II

By Kweli

A GANGSTER'S REVENGE **I II III & IV**

THE BOSS MAN'S DAUGHTERS

THE BOSS MAN'S DAUGHTERS II

THE BOSSMAN'S DAUGHTERS III

THE BOSSMAN'S DAUGHTERS IV

THE BOSS MAN'S DAUGHTERS **V**

A SAVAGE LOVE **I & II**

BAE BELONGS TO ME I II

A HUSTLER'S DECEIT I, II, III

WHAT BAD BITCHES DO I, II, III

SOUL OF A MONSTER I II

KILL ZONE

By **Aryanna**

A KINGPIN'S AMBITON

A KINGPIN'S AMBITION **II**

I MURDER FOR THE DOUGH

By **Ambitious**

TRUE SAVAGE

TRUE SAVAGE II

TRUE SAVAGE **III**

TRUE SAVAGE **IV**

TRUE SAVAGE **V**

TRUE SAVAGE **VI**

By **Chris Green**

A DOPEBOY'S PRAYER

By **Eddie "Wolf" Lee**

THE KING CARTEL **I, II & III**

By **Frank Gresham**

THESE NIGGAS AIN'T LOYAL **I, II & III**

By **Nikki Tee**

GANGSTA SHYT **I II &III**

By **CATO**

THE ULTIMATE BETRAYAL

By **Phoenix**

BOSS'N UP **I , II & III**

By **Royal Nicole**

I LOVE YOU TO DEATH

By Destiny J

I RIDE FOR MY HITTA

I STILL RIDE FOR MY HITTA

By **Misty Holt**

LOVE & CHASIN' PAPER

By **Qay Crockett**

TO DIE IN VAIN

SINS OF A HUSTLA

By **ASAD**

BROOKLYN HUSTLAZ

J-Blunt

220

GOD BLESS THE TRAPPERS I, II, III

THESE SCANDALOUS STREETS I, II, III

FEAR MY GANGSTA I, II, III

THESE STREETS DON'T LOVE NOBODY I, II

BURY ME A G I, II, III, IV, V

A GANGSTA'S EMPIRE I, II, III, IV

THE DOPEMAN'S BODYGAURD

Tranay Adams

THE STREETS ARE CALLING

Duquie Wilson

MARRIED TO A BOSS… I II III

By Destiny Skai & Chris Green

KINGZ OF THE GAME I II III

Playa Ray

SLAUGHTER GANG I II III

RUTHLESS HEART

By Willie Slaughter

THE HEART OF A SAVAGE

By Jibril Williams

FUK SHYT

By Blakk Diamond

DON'T F#CK WITH MY HEART I II

By Linnea

ADDICTED TO THE DRAMA I II III

By Jamila

YAYO

By S. Allen

TRAP GOD

J-Blunt

By Troublesome

BOOKS BY LDP'S CEO, CA$H

TRUST IN NO MAN

TRUST IN NO MAN 2

TRUST IN NO MAN 3

BONDED BY BLOOD

SHORTY GOT A THUG

THUGS CRY

THUGS CRY 2

THUGS CRY 3

TRUST NO BITCH

TRUST NO BITCH 2

TRUST NO BITCH 3

TIL MY CASKET DROPS

RESTRAINING ORDER

RESTRAINING ORDER 2

IN LOVE WITH A CONVICT

Coming Soon

BONDED BY BLOOD 2

BOW DOWN TO MY GANGSTA

J-Blunt